MW01139924

A Spring Sentiment

THE SECOND SEASON OF SERENDIPITY

Elizabeth Ann
WEST

© 2014, Elizabeth Ann West. All rights reserved. To contact the publisher, please write to

41 Silas Deane Road
Ledyard, CT 06339

or email
writer@elizabethannwest.com

ISBN-13: 978-1501077630

ISBN-10: 1501077635

No act of kindness, no matter how small, is ever wasted.

Aesop

Acknowledgments

This series would not be possible without the love and kind support of the Jane Austen Fan Fiction community. I am a proud author member of BeyondAusten.com and Forum.Darcyandlizzy.com. The readers and other authors at both communities make writing in this genre such a joy.

I also want to say a huge thank you to both April Floyd and Betty Madden. These two women help me push my prose to very best it can be, and both are fantastic to work with. I feel so blessed to have both of them on my team.

The readers at TheCheapEbook.com are also wonderful friends of my writing and without them, my launches would fall flat on their faces! The "Piggies" are savvy readers with hearts of gold.

Finally, to my husband who supports me 110%, my super stepson who tells anyone and everyone his mother is an author, and to my five-year-old daughter who insists I do not *write* stories, I *type* them, thank you. Mommy couldn't do this without you. Don't worry Catie, Mommy will write enough stories to take you to see the princesses.

Elizabeth Ann West

ALSO BY ELIZABETH ANN WEST

AUSTEN INSPIRED

The Trouble With Horses
Darcy fell, Elizabeth saves him and the whole town is talking about it! A sweet historical romance novella.

A Winter Wrong
First book in the *Seasons of Serendipity* novella series. When Mr. Bennet dies of an epidemic, Elizabeth Bennet learns that the kindness of a stranger can be quite dashing! A sweet, historical romance novella.

OTHER TITLES

Cancelled
Original novel, a modern romance told mostly from the male point-of-view. A robotics engineer becomes engaged to his perfect match when a previous one-night stand shows up to return his shirt. Pregnant. And it's his.

To Jocelyn, get better my dear friend.

Chapter One

Lydia Bennet moaned on the couch with her arm over her forehead for dramatic effect. Her sister, Kitty Bennet, continued to scribble at the desk by the window in their Aunt Phillips' home, ignoring her younger sister completely. Since losing their father the previous winter, the Bennet family had lost Longbourn and were most uncomfortably scattered across the homes of two relations.

Peeking out from under her forearm, Lydia saw that Kitty hadn't moved so she sighed again and sat up. A bag of chocolates with a pretty bow sat on the table in front of her, one of the many gifts her elder sister Elizabeth enjoyed from her wealthy fiance, Mr. Darcy. Gleefully, Lydia untied the bow and helped herself to the bag.

"Lizzie will be very cross with you."

"Oh, tosh. Mr. Darcy will surely buy her all the chocolates she wants. Besides, I was the first to get engaged, and now no one is excited at all about MY wedding."

Slapping her pen down with force, Kitty finally turned around. "That's because your fiance abandoned his post and ran up debts. He probably isn't coming back you know."

"Yes, he is!" Lydia popped a chocolate into her mouth in defiance.

"No, he's not. Face it, you're damaged goods."

The chocolate in Lydia's mouth tasted odd, and she quickly spat it out. "Ugh, these chocolates are ruined."

Kitty frowned and rose from her chair to walk over and quickly clean up the half-chewed chocolate from the floor with her handkerchief. Carefully tucking the edges around it, she also retied the bow on the chocolates as best she could.

"You know, you really should—"

The door opened and the happy couple, plus the oldest Bennet sister Jane, entered from the cold. Brushing light snow from her beloved's shoulder, Elizabeth was all smiles until she glanced into the parlor.

"Kitty! Those are my chocolates!" Elizabeth marched forward to take them, but Kitty simply handed them to her and returned to the desk. Lydia made a face at Kitty and flounced back onto the couch. Blowing out a breath to warm her hands, Kitty picked up her pen and continued to write, eviscerating her youngest sister in fiction. Kitty had found solace and relief in writing since the unexpected passing of their father.

Jane gently patted Lydia's legs to make the young girl sit up again as she had resumed lying on the couch out of cheek.

"No, Miss Bennet, 'tis unnecessary. I am afraid I must go." Mr. Darcy announced. Elizabeth pouted until Darcy gave her one of his grim smiles. "Mr.

Bingley is set to arrive this evening and I would like to be at Netherfield to receive him."

"La, how droll that you are master of Netherfield more than Mr. Bingley when he holds the lease."

"Lydia!" Jane and Elizabeth admonished at once. Cries from Mrs. Bennet came from upstairs, and within seconds, the widow Bennet was thundering down the steps in full mourning attire.

"Oh, Mr. Darcy, how delighted we are with your company! Did I hear correctly? You have brought Mr. Bingley back for my dear Jane?"

Mr. Darcy cleared his throat and looked away. It always took him a moment or two to disguise his visceral reactions to Mrs. Bennet before he could respond.

"Mama, Mr. Darcy did not need to bring Mr. Bingley back as his plans were to always return to Hertfordshire. He had business to attend in London and merely could not travel with us," Elizabeth explained and rolled her eyes. Two weeks returned from her uncle's house in Cheapside and already her own mother tried her nerves. Taking pity on her dear Darcy, Elizabeth offered to show him out.

Outside, the light snow flurries continued to fall. A soft crunching sound echoed as they walked towards the stables so that Mr. Darcy could fetch his horse, Poseidon. Once the groom was out of sight, Mr. Darcy bent down and quickly kissed the tip of Elizabeth's nose. Instantly burning with a blush, Elizabeth turned away.

"Mr. Darcy!"

"William," he answered, in a soft voice.

Elizabeth took a breath and turned back around.

"William," she repeated.

"I would, that is, I would like it if we could use our Christian names when we are in private, Elizabeth."

The way he said her name made her tingle all the way down to her toes, though it wasn't the first time she had heard it. Before she could respond, the groom was walking the horse towards them.

"Why did you. . ." she started and then stopped, realizing she could not voice her question within the range of the groom's hearing.

Mr. Darcy took the reins from the young man and mounted. He looked down at Elizabeth and gave her one his rare smiles. "You had a snowflake on your nose."

As the horse galloped away, Elizabeth wrapped her shawl tighter around her shoulders and watched until William disappeared into the gray horizon. She silently prayed that no harm would come to Mr. Darcy while riding home in the snow, and as she heard more shrill voices from inside break the chilly peace around her, she added a quick request for deliverance from her family if the Lord would be so benevolent.

Mr. Darcy and Mr. Bingley called the following day, and the two gentlemen agreed to a walk into Meryton with the two oldest Bennet sisters. Talk still had not died down about Mr. Wickham's apparent desertion from the militia, nor his abandoning Lydia, but Mr. Darcy had at least taken care of the outstanding debts. As the couples walked, they ran into another new couple of Meryton, Mr. and Mrs. Collins.

For a moment, the three couples said nothing until Charlotte Collins broke the ice.

"What a lovely gown, Lizzie! Green is a most becoming color on you. I've been meaning to call since I heard you were in town."

Elizabeth smiled. "I would like that very much! So much has changed . . ."

"Indeed," Charlotte responded.

When another icy silence descended, the ladies curtsied, but the men did not bow. Before long, Charlotte and Mr. Collins were gone, and everyone could breathe more easily.

Just as they reached the end of town, which was a much shorter walk from Elizabeth's Aunt Philips' home than her childhood home that was now owned by Mr. Collins, Mr. Darcy spoke in a low tone so that only Elizabeth could hear him. "I would prefer to be present when Mrs. Collins comes to call."

"Charlotte? Oh, she's been a dear friend for ages. I hardly think Mr. Collins will call as well."

"Be that as it may, I will attend you the next few days during the appropriate hours so that I may be party."

Elizabeth set her mouth and pursed her lips. Carefully weighing a number of responses, she devised a plan and very politely smiled at her William. "As you wish, Mr. Darcy. Now, I believe we have arrived?"

The two couples were at the office of her Uncle Phillips to discuss a very serious matter: the future living accommodations for Mrs. Bennet and the remaining Bennet daughters.

"Gentlemen, gentlemen, come in!" Andrew Phillips greeted the two suitors most enthusiastically. Being the only solicitor in town, he was a jack of all trades; from real estate holdings to wills, Mr. Phillips handled it all.

Elizabeth and Jane mostly listened as the three properties were discussed in great detail. The Smith House ruled out as a recent fire would require costly reparations, there were only two acceptable domiciles left in the area to lease. It was to be either the old Winslow Manor, located on the far side of the woods next to Longbourn, or Fenley Cottage, a smaller home with charming windows, closer to town. The clear favorite was the cottage with a cost savings of nearly two hundred pounds per annum.

"I'm not certain Mama will enjoy thinking of her home with the savings in mind," Jane sweetly advised.

Mr. Bingley leaned back in his chair while her uncle leaned forward to pat her hand.

"Fanny hates any mention of budgeting, but it is what must be done. She cannot continue to live in the lifestyle she was accustomed to before your esteemed father passed."

Jane frowned and looked at Elizabeth, who pretended to inspect an errant thread on her dress skirt. Neither sister was ignorant of her mother's ways, and the following day's viewing of both properties was going to be quite the trial. It was decided that the Bingley and Darcy carriages would be used to take the whole family for the outing.

Once they returned to the Phillips' home, the gentlemen had to plead their absence at the request they remain for dinner. Elizabeth was relieved as the table was already quite cramped with five Bennets squeezing in with two Phillipses.

"I will instruct Caroline to plan a dinner very soon. She is much fatigued from yesterday's travel, but yes, I suspect before the week is out we shall all dine together at Netherfield." Mr. Bingley offered, to the great delight of Mrs. Bennet.

While everyone remained distracted by the joyous raptures of her mother and the attention of Mr. Bingley, Elizabeth spoke to Mr. Darcy in a very low voice, much as he had employed earlier in Meryton.

"What is she doing here?"

Mr. Darcy did not look at Elizabeth, so none might know they were talking, and instead pretended to mind the other conversation going on between Mr. Bingley and the Bennets. "I had no say in the matter; apparently Bingley failed to dissuade her insistence on visiting Netherfield."

Elizabeth was livid as a green, slithery monster by the name of jealousy writhed within her heart. She was suddenly very keen that Mr. Darcy spend every afternoon with her, despite his high-handed ways, though that didn't mean she was going to abandon her plans to teach him a lesson when Charlotte came calling.

"I shall send a note to Charlotte to visit next Monday. Would that be convenient for you?"

Mr. Darcy merely nodded. He and Charles were finally able to extricate themselves from the house with Mrs. Bennet seeing them to the door. There was no call for Elizabeth to see Mr. Darcy out, though memories of yesterday's farewell brought an involuntary blush to her cheeks. Her face rosy with love, she locked eyes with Mr. Darcy as he donned his hat and quickly ducked out of the house.

Elizabeth hurried to the window to watch as he rode away. Once her vigilance was satisfied, she picked up her sewing basket and resumed stitching the initials E.D. and F.D. intertwined on a set of handkerchiefs she planned to give to Mr. Darcy in honor of their marriage. She didn't realize she was humming until Lydia made such a racket to demand that she stop.

Chapter Two

Poor weather delayed the planned outing for inspection of proper housing for the Bennet women all week. But by Thursday morning, an invitation to dine at Netherfield arrived as the roads were just barely dry enough for the carriage to travel the short distance.

With a heavy heart, Elizabeth sighed while the carriage passed Longbourn. Squished to the window while sharing a bench with Kitty and Lydia, she found looking out at the passing landscape the only available position of comfort.

"This carriage smells of beets." Lydia wrinkled her nose in response to her own observation.

"It was very kind of Mr. Darcy to purchase the old Long carriage for our use, Lydia. You be sure to thank him." Mrs. Bennet scolded.

"Me? That's Lizzie's job." Lydia rolled her eyes.

Elizabeth ignored the bait to allow Lydia a discussion about how she could thank Mr. Darcy and continued staring out the window. She could just make out her favorite path up to Oakham Mount in the dwindling light.

"Mama, when do you think I might purchase

more paper? I am nearly without."

"Gracious, child, you know we are on economy. Your writing is a hobby we may not be able to afford very much longer!"

"But Lydia bought new ribbon and fabric! It's not fair!"

"And when you're engaged to be married, you can buy new ribbon and fabric, too," Lydia responded with a mocking voice.

"Mama!"

"Girls! Girls! My nerves!" Mrs. Bennet began to flutter her handkerchief and breathe in and out at a rapid rate. Jane reached over to pat her mother's hand.

"You're not even engaged anymore. He left you!"

"No, he didn't! He has business in London. Take that back!" Lydia grabbed Kitty's arm and pinched with a twist.

"Ow! Mama!" Kitty swatted back at Lydia.

Jostled about and hitting her forehead on the glass, Elizabeth turned toward her sisters and grabbed Lydia and Kitty by their arms, pinning them to the back of the bench. "Cease this moment! So help me, I will open that carriage door and cast you both out!" Elizabeth stared her sisters down and finally released them. Making sure her dress was properly adjusted, Elizabeth took a calming breath. "Kitty, I will take you into town tomorrow to purchase paper. You must stop antagonizing Lydia, and do not dare hint at Wickham during this dinner."

Meekly, the two youngest girls shrank back from their older sister. It was rare to see Lizzie flare up in temper, and for a time they modified their behavior. The carriage remained silent as it creaked and groaned up the drive to Netherfield.

Ever practiced at recovering from a sisterly squabble, the Bennet sisters descended from the equipage as though nothing fractious had occurred. The ladies were greeted by two dashing gentlemen on the stairs, eager to escort them inside. As Bingley walked forward to claim Mrs. Bennet's arm; Darcy was free to claim his betrothed.

"Miss Elizabeth." Darcy bowed deeply and offered to take her arm. The estate aglow in soft candlelight, Elizabeth wondered how Netherfield compared to the illustrious Pemberley.

"Do you miss your home very much, sir?" she asked as they carefully traversed the worn and slightly icy steps to the front entrance.

"Indeed, but not nearly so much as I would miss you if I was apart from your company."

Elizabeth's brilliant smile and laughter with Mr. Darcy made Caroline Bingley freeze in the foyer. She had half-heartedly put together this dinner after much debate with her brother. The more she saw Darcy with that plain chit of a girl, the more certain she became that she only need show him what an upstart Elizabeth was, and then she could win him back. She refused to believe her brother's constant warnings that Darcy had never held a romantic interest in her.

"How lucky, dinner is ready to be served!" Caroline walked forward to claim Mr. Darcy's other arm.

"Caroline, they have only just arrived. Surely we are to take drinks in the drawing room first," Mr. Bingley said through his teeth.

Caroline waved her hand dismissively at her

brother. "I cannot be responsible if the cooks in these backwater counties cannot stick to a simple schedule. I was just informed that dinner is ready to be served, and I am sure the courses would be ruined if we wait."

With barely enough time to have their cloaks removed by footmen, the Bennet family entered the formal dining room to a very bizarre table setting. On the one end, there was a plate flanked by two, with the entire middle of the table left empty. On the opposite end, there was a plate flanked by two pair. Clearly, the intent was for the Bennet family to dine at one end of the table, alone.

"Who placed these settings?" Caroline yelled out making the kitchen staff in the dining room suddenly disappear through the door towards the kitchen in search of various tasks, except for a lone footman who dared to point out that Caroline herself had given instruction for the odd setting.

Elizabeth couldn't hide her smile at the footman's breach and looked at Kitty, who also pulled a face, making Elizabeth laugh aloud. "Fret not, Miss Bingley! Perhaps you have yet to master clearly communicating with your staff. It can be difficult for those not raised in such a household" She broke off from Mr. Darcy's arm and calmly picked up a plate to carry to the side of the table with only three. Each of her sisters took the hint, and Lydia grabbed two plates to include their mother.

"Oh, that's much better! What a, er, lovely centerpiece you have, Miss Bingley!" Mrs. Bennet struggled to find a compliment for the young woman as Caroline was escorted to the very end of the table by Mr. Darcy. For his part, after dropping

Miss Bingley at her seat, instead of taking the setting next to her, he and Kitty whipped around the table to change places so he was across from Miss Bingley, but sitting next to Elizabeth's right side to round out the seating.

While the footman served each guest, Mr. Bingley kept the chatter going as he delighted Kitty and Lydia with tales of London. Loose plans were made to visit various exhibitions and the famed Covent Gardens when the warm weather returned.

"Please, Mama, can't we all go to London in the spring? It would be such a diversion!" Lydia exclaimed.

"Forgive me, but I thought you were soon to be married. Married women rarely have time for such activities, or so my sister is always telling me." Caroline gave a knowing smile to Lydia as she took a sip of wine.

"I am not—"

"We have not set our plans for the spring just yet. Mr. Darcy, we have not yet decided where we are to wed! Would you prefer to return to Pemeberley or have the ceremony in London?" Elizabeth interrupted and changed the subject.

Mr. Darcy frowned at the obviously mean behavior of his friend's sister. It wasn't until Elizabeth gently touched his arm that he was shaken out of his own thoughts about how to keep the woman away from his impressionable younger sister, Georgiana.

"Mr. Darcy?"

"Yes, forgive me; I was not attending."

"I was just asking about your thoughts for our wedding. Where would you like it to take place?" Elizabeth hid a laugh by tucking her bottom lip under her top one with a wide smile.

"You must have it here in Meryton, of course! We will have the grandest wedding breakfast the county has ever seen. Perhaps you and Jane could make it a double wedding. Wouldn't that be nice, Lizzie?" Mrs. Bennet cooed and nodded in approval to her own plan.

Jane and Bingley both blushed, and it was Jane who softly reminded her mother that she and Mr. Bingley were not engaged.

"Well, with so many daughters, and two recently engaged, it is not a wonder that you lost track, Mrs. Bennet." Caroline said, her face a studied mock of sympathy.

Ignoring Caroline, Mrs. Bennett addressed Jane instead, "Er, well, yes, I suppose. I merely get carried away when it's obvious you and Mr. Bingley are so violently in love. Anyone can see that. Yes, that's it."

The table was uncomfortably quiet as, besides Mrs. Bennet, the entire party suddenly became interested in their plates. It was a few moments before Elizabeth realized Mr. Darcy had never answered her about where they were to be married, and worse than that, she realized she didn't have a wedding date. She knew they were waiting to hear from Colonel Fitzwilliam about the search for Wickham, but it had been three weeks already. What if the man was never found? Would Darcy call off their engagement?

As conversation swirled around her, Elizabeth was lost in the dour mood that had lately latched onto her mind. Whenever talk of her wedding arose, so did the thought of her father. She had always dreamt of the day he would walk her down the aisle. And now, she might not even have a wedding if Mr.

Wickham couldn't be found and made to marry Lydia. She felt her eyes growing moist as a heaviness threatened to descend on her heart. It was only when Mr. Darcy nudged her that she realized Mr. Bingley was speaking to her.

"I said, Miss Elizabeth, that you had high hopes for the cottage, did you not, as being the perfect home for your mother and sisters?"

Elizabeth shook her head and looked to Jane, but couldn't catch her eye. Jane was looking at her lap, and Elizabeth felt uncomfortable being used as a pawn in Mr. Bingley and Mr. Darcy's attempt to convince her mother into a smaller house.

"I fear I must suspend my preferences until we can view the properties, sir." Elizabeth smiled meekly.

"Then we must all go tomorrow! It will be a party, and we could pack a picnic!" Miss Bingley offered with a catty smile.

"Miss Bingley, thank you, but no. My mother cannot possibly enjoy a picnic in her mourning state and the weather is hardly warm enough for a stroll, let alone a picnic." Jane surprised Elizabeth by finally speaking her mind to the woman who would be her sister-in-law if Bingley would just get on with it and ask Jane to marry him.

"I completely forgot, forgive me. It's just that you and your sisters ran around London so much this winter, I wasn't sure you were even observing a proper mourning period."

"Caroline!" Mr. Bingley admonished.

But it was Elizabeth who cleared her throat. "My sisters and I may not have had the security afforded to you when you lost your parents and had a brother to take you in, Miss Bingley, but my father would be very proud that his daughters did not dally about crying hay while our futures were so unstable."

Caroline sniffed and replied, "You are so decidedly sure of your opinions, Miss Eliza. That is such a refreshing trait to possess."

A sudden clanging of metal rang from behind the door and Caroline threw her napkin on the table. "What now?" she exclaimed as she rose from the table, causing Mr. Darcy and Mr. Bingley to immediately rise with her to the sound of scraping chairs on the wooden floor. They both remained standing and only resumed their seats after she made her way to the servant's door.

The dinner party flinched as Miss Bingley's shouts and abuse could be heard through the door. Elizabeth continued to work on her second course and took a healthy gulp of wine. Conversation remained stilted until Miss Bingley finally reappeared.

"It would seem that terrible crash was the rest of our dinner as James' clumsiness set off a chain of falls down the stairs. I'm afraid dinner is at an end."

Mr. Bingley turned a bright shade of red as he held his breath before finally erupting. "Caroline Margaret Bingley, this is beyond the pale! You go down to that kitchen, and I don't care if you have to help prepare it yourself, but there will be cold meats and fruit served in the drawing room in fifteen minutes." Mr. Bingley rose and offered an arm to Mrs. Bennet, who gladly accepted such gallant behavior. "I'm terribly sorry, Mrs. Bennet; I'm afraid tonight's dinner has been a complete disaster."

"Ohhh, nothing to fret about, Mr. Bingley. Your sister is very young. It is difficult to hold such events as these without the proper training. I made sure to instruct all of my girls. . .," Mrs. Bennet continued to chat about the various admirable qualities of Jane and her other daughters as Mr. Bingley caught Jane's arm and escorted the ladies to the hall. Kitty and Lydia followed closely behind as they had finished their meal, their laughter and chatter grating on Caroline's nerves as they glanced back at her.

"Mr. Darcy, I— ,"

Darcy held up a hand to stop Caroline's attempt at redemption as he offered to escort Miss Elizabeth. "Truly, Miss Bingley, your motives were rather transparent."

Leaving Miss Bingley in the dining room, Elizabeth and Darcy found themselves alone in the foyer as the rest of the party had retired to the drawing room. Mr. Darcy tried to stop as Elizabeth walked on, until his sudden halt pulled her back to step in line next to him.

"Elizabeth. . .," he muttered, turning her to him.

"Do not, sir. Please desist with your pretty words and caresses."

Suddenly shocked out of his arduous mood, Mr. Darcy furrowed his brow. "What's this? Have I done something to offend you?"

"Not at all, sir. Your silence was most agreeable." Elizabeth unlinked her arm from Mr. Darcy and walked the remaining steps to the drawing room. Just as she was to turn the knob and open the door, Darcy grabbed her hand and pulled her around to follow him behind the staircase. The jerk was so sudden and unexpected, Elizabeth followed without resistance.

"Mr. Darcy, we cannot be away from the others."

"We are already engaged, Elizabeth. Now, please,

before Caroline Bingley's petty behavior further ruins the evening, will you not tell me what vexes you?"

"You! All through dinner, you were silent. Not until the end did you say anything to that harpy-"

"That harpy who is my hostess while I remain here."

"Yes, but—but you said nothing when I asked about our wedding date!"

Mr. Darcy took a step back as they had become very close in their heated discussion. He covered his mouth with his hand and dragged the skin as he rubbed his chin. Finally, he placed both hands on Elizabeth's arms and looked deep into her eyes.

"There are some subjects which I am never inclined to discuss in front of others and I consider our wedding plans to be a most private matter for only you and me to discuss."

"Pray, when do you intend to discuss these plans with me, privately?"

Darcy let go of her arms and walked away. "As soon as we may arrange, madam."

Elizabeth stood for a moment before scurrying to catch up to him. The way that man could make her heart melt in one moment and infuriate her in the next was most taxing! This love business was absolutely exhausting.

She took his arm and silently slipped into the drawing room to find Lydia entertaining the group with a funny story that was clearly embarrassing Kitty. Taking a deep breath, Elizabeth released it slowly in frustration that she would have to keep a vigilant eye on those two for the remainder of the evening. The dinner at Netherfield couldn't end soon enough for her taste, even if her stomach was still rumbling in hunger.

❧ ❧ ❧ ❧ ❧ ❧ ❧ ❧ ❧

The dingy, dirty streets of London were a natural hiding place for the unwashed who preferred not to be found. Mr. George Wickham, lately of the militia, stumbled out of a gambling den with coins jingling in his pocket, belching from heavy drink. His eyes struggled to focus on the signs around him, and he turned around a few times to look in all directions for the alleyway he had come in on.

"George Wickham. Fancy seeing you again." A familiar woman's voice called out to him in the mist. He shakily stumbled forward with a lopsided grin on his face.

"Sally Younge! What brings a good girl like you out here on a night like this?"

"Just looking for boarders. I run a house around the corner. Warm bed. Clean linens."

"Awww, you offering me a place for old times' sake?" He gallantly placed his arm around her shoulder as she began steering him toward the far corner of the street.

"Old times nothing. You pay, just like everybody else!" She threw his arm off as her boots made crisp, curt connections with the stone steps to her run-down row house. She stopped on the top step and looked back. Wickham held the railing and swayed gently in his drunkenness.

"How's about I pay the way I used to?"

Sally Younge laughed. "You're too far gone for that, but come inside all's the same. You won't be freezing on my front doorstep."

Mr. Wickham tipped his shabby hat and lurched forward with assistance from the railing. Using a wide gait, he managed to stumble up the steps and into the meager warmth of the tenement before Mrs. Younge, the former companion to Miss Georgiana Darcy, shut the heavy wooden door against the chill.

Chapter Three

Elizabeth Bennet skipped down the three flattish stones that she considered to be the steps of Oakham Mount. The morning was bright and cool with the scent of dew in the air. She had absconded from her aunt's home for a much needed escape. The smokestacks of Longbourn puffing in the distance, she felt tears well up as she greatly missed her former life. Coming back to Hertfordshire was a daily trial in keeping her emotions regulated, and living a life in limbo between pitied orphan and married woman was doing little to quell her inner turmoil.

The familiar sound of horse hooves thundering down the road made Elizabeth smile in spite of herself. Last night at the disastrous Netherfield dinner, she and her betrothed had made a tenuous agreement to meet surreptitiously. Hastily, she wiped her eyes of any sign of tears and pinched her chilled cheeks for good measure.

The horse slowed as it neared and she heard the rider jump down from the mount. As she turned, her bonnet was caught in a February gust and fell to hang around her neck. She giggled at Mr. Darcy's sudden gasp at her undress, covering her mouth with a gloved hand.

"Good morning, Mr. Darcy. What a delight to encounter you during my morning walk." Elizabeth bowed her head into a curtsy.

"Well, at least this time you're not falling out of a tree." Darcy linked his arm with hers as poor Poseidon once again was forced to endure their human pace.

"Jumping, William. I jumped out of that tree." She looked up at him without the intrusion of her bonnet and laughed. "And I make no promises as to the future inspection of trees at Pemberley, sir."

After a moment, Darcy cleared his throat. "I may be able to show you one or two great climbers." He looked down and winked at her, causing Elizabeth to blush and bump into his side for his tease with her hip.

As the turn for Longbourn came, the two continued to walk on past and Darcy noticed Elizabeth's shoulders tensing. "I believe, madam, that we have yet to discuss our nuptials. And while I would prefer they had occurred yesterday, perhaps we had better agree upon a date?" Elizabeth sighed. She did wish to discuss these matters as they'd dined at Netherfield, but with the day's dawning she wasn't sure what to say with everything up in the air regarding her family. Should she marry before Lydia? Would that make the gossip worse? Would it be best to wait a full year from her father's passing? Where would her mother and sisters live?

"I am afraid you've caught me once again unsure of my wishes, though I know I baited you almost past your patience last evening. What are your thoughts, sir?"

Darcy couldn't believe his ears. As he slowed his walk, Poseidon's muzzle bumped into his back reminding him to march on. "We could start reading the banns here in Meryton. I'm sure Reverend Willoughby would do an admirable job."

Elizabeth frowned. "No, I cannot say I desire to be married from home." Gritting his teeth, Darcy responded that clearly she did have wishes he was at a loss to postulate. "Truly I did not have a preference until you mentioned the possibility! But the idea of being married in the church where I grew up, where I was baptized, with my father out in the..."

"Forgive me, I did not consider—" Darcy began as Elizabeth stubbornly swiped at tears that would not cease.

"I'm afraid this maudlin mood appears far too often these days, and without my approval." Elizabeth took a deep breath and blew it out. The tension in her neck and shoulders began to release. "Perhaps I was too hasty, William. I would like to see my mother settled and then we can return to London. My Aunt and Uncle Gardiner are most important to me. London would be the easiest ceremony for our families to attend. . ."

Darcy raised an eyebrow at his beautiful future wife. "Are you certain you would like things to be unsettled until then? I can mount Poseidon as we speak and hie to London for a special license. At your command, of course, Elizabeth."

Laughing, Elizabeth shook her head. She stopped their progress and tentatively raised an arm to touch not Mr. Darcy, but Poseidon. The horse snorted into her gloved hand, but allowed her to stroke his muzzle. "As much as I know this gentleman would fancy a great gallop, I'm afraid I'm a bit partial to his rider. I do not think I could bear to be separated." Her eyes looked up to meet his, and for a moment, the haunting loneliness they both carried was acknowledged.

Poseidon's whinny broke the spell and now coming up on Aunt Phillips' home, they could hear the sounds of the rising Bennet family. A stable boy bounded up to take the reins of Poseidon and lead him away.

Before they could walk in, Elizabeth held back. "I have a request, and I was wondering if you might be willing . . . that is . . ." Elizabeth nibbled on her bottom lip as she worried how he might take this solicitation given they were not yet married.

"Miss Elizabeth Bennet, you need only ask. If it is within my power, I shall make it so." Mr. Darcy said gallantly in his Master of Pemberley voice that she had once mistaken to mean he was so proud.

"There is a maid employed at Netherfield, and with our future plans including travel to London and beyond, I would very much like her by my side."

Darcy smiled as he recalled the young maid at Netherfield, "Ah, Becky. Say no more; I believe that an excellent idea, and I will discuss the particulars with Bingley. As long as Miss Bingley does not become acquainted with the details, I do not anticipate a problem for the maid to travel with us to London."

Elizabeth sighed her relief and together they entered a home in a complete uproar. "Lizzie Bennet, there you are! Oh, good morning, Mr. Darcy!" Mrs. Bennet snapped at Elizabeth, but modulated her tone to greet her future son-in-law. "Lydia and Kitty are both ill. What a day for the girls to fall ill, when we are to view the two properties most graciously selected by Mr. Darcy and Mr. Bingley! Don't those girls have more sense?"

Elizabeth tried tempering her mother's bluster, "Mama, I'm sure Lydia and Kitty do not mean to be ill."

Elizabeth and Darcy followed Mrs. Bennet to the table for breakfast. Elizabeth greeted her Aunt Phillips and invited Darcy to join them with a wave of her hand. Her mother hovered before taking the seat Mr. Darcy had readied for her. "The day is ruined. And I was so looking forward to viewing the properties. I suppose we shall have to trespass upon you, dear sister, a little while longer." Mrs. Bennet reached and took the cup of tea Elizabeth had just prepared for Mr. Darcy. Gaping at her mother's manners, yet wary of provoking yet more of her onslaught, silently Elizabeth turned to prepare another cup of tea. For her part, Aunt Phillips blanched and resumed focus on her toast.

Darcy cleared his throat. "While I am sorry to hear that Miss Lydia and Miss Kitty are indisposed, I do not think there is any harm in allowing your remaining daughters to escort you to the properties, Mrs. Bennet. I do not believe the younger ladies will have the wisdom of your experience in running a household, and it is that experience that will be most helpful in selecting a suitable property." Mrs. Bennet sat up straighter and batted her eyelashes at Mr. Darcy, causing Elizabeth to roll her eyes behind her mother. She caught Mr. Darcy's gaze and smirked as the two of them shared an unspoken communication. The sooner Fanny Bennet was settled, the sooner they could be on their way to London.

❧ ❧ ❧ ❧ ❧ ❧ ❧ ❧ ❧

Lady Matlock rang the bell and the red door to Darcy House opened to admit her entrance. She allowed the butler to remove her wrap and cocked her head to one side to hear the delightful sounds of young women laughing above. Shaking her head, she made a shooing motion with her hands to Mr. Marlborough to eschew a formal announcement. Instead, the grand lady ascended the steps to the main floor and stopped just outside the music room.

"You've much improved, Mary! Play that trill again!" Mary Bennet furrowed her brow, her tongue slightly peeking from between her tightly pulled lips. With great effort, she repeated the complicated Mozart piece and ended with a flourish.

"Oh, bravo! Bravo!" Lady Matlock clapped from the doorway and finally entered. Mary folded her hands into her lap and blushed while Georgiana smiled and greeted her aunt. "You ladies have been busy! Good for you, Miss Mary."

"Thank you, mi'lady." Mary did not seek out Lady Matlock's gaze but instead kept her eyes on the piano forte.

"What brings you here, Aunt? Are we to go shopping?" Georgiana Darcy perked up and followed her aunt to the settee. Lady Matlock took a seat and looked Mary Bennet up and down. Yes, the young woman's attire had greatly improved from the first time they'd met, but her confidence was grievously lacking. Lady Matlock clucked her tongue at her own thoughts.

"Aunt?" Georgiana looked confused until she

followed her aunt's gaze to Mary and then looked back at the older woman.

"I have decided that while Fitzwilliam is off running around in your home county, Miss Mary, and my own son is running around doing who knows what for the War Office, I have a need for company. I would like to invite you and my niece to come stay at Matlock House for a few weeks, so we may become better acquainted.

"Oh, Aunt, that sounds lovely! What do you think, Mary? Aunt Maggie's house is wonderful. There's a larger garden, and we can work on. . . well, you know."

Lady Matlock gave Mary an amused look. "What are you two plotting?"

Mary sucked in her breath, then answered. "At home, we made our own rose water and lavender balm. I was hoping to make a set for my sister for her wedding."

Lady Matlock laughed. "Oh, dear, we can simply buy those in Mayfair!"

"Yes, milady, we could . . ." Mary struggled for a moment out of fear of offending Lady Matlock, but decided her honestly would be welcome, "but I believe my sister will appreciate the effort."

"Oh, yes, of course she will! What do we need for this little aromatic adventure? Bottles? Presses?" Georgiana and Mary looked at each other and grinned. With Lady Matlock on their side, they could make the wedding gift doubly fine!

Chapter Four

George Wickham slammed the door to the small boarding house run by Sally Younge, causing Mrs. Younge and the maid she was instructing to flinch. Mrs. Younge dismissed the maid to continue her duties, and with a frown, she approached the young rake now helping himself to brandy in her sitting room.

Swiping the bottle from him, she gave him a stern glare and placed the bottle on a side table. As she approached him, George Wickham collapsed into an armchair, gulping the brandy he'd managed to pour into a glass lest she take that away, too.

"So? What information did you find?"

"It's useless. The young girls were spirited away to Matlock House just as I grew close enough to weasel my way in. Darcy is out in Hertfordshire. Can't lurk out there. Too many would recognize me." Wickham finished his drink and carelessly let the cup drop from his hand to the floor with a clatter.

With a swish of skirts, Sally Younge snatched the glass from the floor and shoved his legs off the table where he had reclined them. "You ain't quite current on the bill here. Have a mind not to consider yourself too comfortable like."

"I'm ruined. Throw me out tomorrow. Throw me out tonight. There's no difference, madam."

Returning the brandy and glass to its proper place, Sally took a moment to consider the situation. She'd seen Wickham fall into his depressive moods before. He was in such a state last summer when she'd coaxed him into trying to elope with Georgiana Darcy. This time the revenge was for both of them.

"You'll just have to think of another way to get at him. You're always so clever, there must be some way. . .," she trailed off.

"It's useless. My only hope was to grab one of the girls, either Georgiana or that scripture speaking Mary, as collateral. But with Lydia out of reach, they'll never have her marry me now."

Sally Younge frowned as the young maid returned from answering the door and handed her mistress a card. The widow laughed as she read and turned her eyes back to the bounder in her parlor. "Looks like you can earn your keep while we figure out a new plan. Mrs. Clayton finds she has need for a companion this evening."

"Not the fat one, Sally girl! Her dogs yip and yap something awful." Wickham continued his pout from the chair, and Mrs. Younge dismissed the maid.

Taking one finger to run up his arm to his shoulder and to finally rise up and caress around the edge of his ear, she felt his body tense at the attention. "Come now, Georgie. You give Mrs. Clayton some friendly attention, and I'll only keep half of what you take in."

"A quarter."

"Half, and that only be beginning to make a dent

in what you owe me."

Realizing he had no choice, George Wickham took the card from Sally and bowed. She clucked her tongue, and he replaced his dour expression with his normal charming demeanor. Giving her a peck on the cheek, he grabbed his hat and left the house, on his way two blocks over to earn his keep.

৵৬ ৵৬ ৵৬ ৵৬ ৵৬ ৵৬ ৵৬ ৵৬ ৵৬

After a week of sleeping in a strange bed, Mary Bennet's eyes popped open in the darkness for the seventh night. The initial panic of wondering where she was abated within a moment, but this time she wasn't still groggy. Allowing her eyes to adjust, the coals in the fire and moonlight spilling in from her window overlooking the courtyard granted her enough illumination to light the candle on her bedside table. Gingerly, she tested the floor boards and sucked in her breath as her bare feet objected to the coolness until she could find her slippers.

Donning her robe, she felt confident she could find the library. She hated to admit it, but the novels Georgiana was introducing to her were far more enjoyable than the sermons she used to read. She mostly enjoyed passing moral judgment on the heroines in the novels and determining the exact moment when their decisions led to their folly.

The dark wooden door to the library was ajar and light seeped out into the hall. When Mary pushed the door open, she saw the fire was still fairly healthy as though it had been recently tended and a number of candelabras remained lit on the tables.

"Hello? Lord Matlock? Lady Matlock?" Mary asked timidly in the night's quiet. With no response, she tiptoed into the room and closed the door behind her.

She didn't take but five steps when a large snore made her nearly jump out of her skin. She couldn't help it, but she called out, and the snorer began a frantic snorting as he awoke and popped his head up from the sofa in front of the fire. Mary covered her mouth to prevent a further scream and the hand holding her candle trembled most fiercely.

Colonel Fitzwilliam rubbed his eyes and looked at the vision before him of Mary Bennet with her hair loose and her porcelain features hauntingly beautiful in the candlelight. "Miss Mary. Good evening." He cleared his throat of the last congestion from sleep interrupted.

"I-I, good evening, sir." She quickly curtsied. "I came for a novel, but clearly I've disturbed you. Please forgive me." She curtsied again and turned to leave.

"Wait!"

Her hand on the door knob, Mary let out a sigh. This was just like those silly novels she had been reading. Every voice in her principled mind screamed she should open the door and not look back. This was that moment that would be her downfall. Instead, her heart smiled and told her to have an adventure for once. Besides, no one would believe that the pious Mary would sneak to a secret meeting with a man in a library in the middle of the night. "Colonel, this is highly irregular. I really shouldn't stay."

The colonel rose from the sofa and tugged on his regimental coat. "Miss Mary, you can trust that I will behave as the perfect gentleman. This is my mother's house, and I would never dare to dishonor her or her guests, and never a lady as gentle as you. I simply didn't want you to run away from me."

Mary's heart melted a little as she took a good long look at the man who was cousin to her future brother-in-law. He was tall and a built fighter. She found his face to display a hardened look she suspected served more to protect his private feelings than to actually reflect a granite heart. "I cannot sleep. I suppose I can sit for a few moments with you."

The Colonel smiled. "We are two of the same. I can rarely fall asleep in my own bed. Mrs. Henry swears the maids love that they need never to tighten my ropes, but the footmen hate the mess I make when I fall asleep with a drink in my hand, or worse, a cigar." He laughed lightly.

"You really mustn't! What if you burn the house down?"

The Colonel shrugged. "If you'd seen what I have, you wouldn't be so hasty to judge." He handed her a small pour of brandy and Mary sniffed at it. "Never had the stronger stuff, eh?" She shook her head. "Well, sip slowly," he said as he sat in the arm chair to allow her space on the sofa.

Mary took another sniff and raised the glass to her lips. Just barely allowing the amber liquid to wet her tongue, she pulled back and made a sour face. The colonel laughed. "It tastes better with practice."

For a few moments they were quiet as Mary was at a loss for words. Here she was in a grand library with a dashing man, alone, at night. Her mind was busy wondering what her mother and sisters would think about such a situation when finally, the colonel broke the silence.

"You know why I can't sleep. What causes your insomnia?"

She shrugged. "Since Papa died, I haven't had a full night's rest. I was never his favorite, nor Mama's, but so much has changed . . ., I don't ever feel safe."

The colonel nodded, which surprised Mary. She expected him to laugh at her again.

"You are wise beyond your years, Miss Mary." The colonel took another large gulp of his own drink, prompting Mary to try another sip of hers. This time her tongue was better prepared, and she could taste the sweetness after the burn.

"Mr. Wickham is dangerous, isn't he?"

The colonel's eyes widened. "Like I said, wise beyond your years." He lifted his glass to toast her cleverness.

"That's why we're here. Lady Matlock didn't truly desire my company." She twisted her mouth wistfully and looked down at her lap. The colonel reached forward and lightly touched her hand. Startled, she looked up at him and after a moment, gently moved her hand away.

"My family admires you very much, Miss Mary. The fact that you are here for your safety bespeaks just how much my mother cares for your well-being. You don't see other young ladies of London invited, do you?"

Mary immediately let out a small laugh, followed by more giggles. Setting her glass on the table in front of the sofa with most of the liquid still in it, she rose from the sofa.

"I think I will be able to sleep now."

The colonel nodded and watched as the young woman retrieved her candle and left the library. Yawning and stretching, he finished off the last of her drink and blew out the candles, except for the one he took with him. He would sleep in his own bed tonight, if only to make sure there'd be no talk if one of the servants had seen Mary enter or exit the library. If they had, the last thing he wanted for himself or the lady was for him to be found in the morning, snoring on the sofa.

❧ ❧ ❧ ❧ ❧ ❧ ❧ ❧ ❧

The Gardiner household was very quiet without the Bennet girls and Madeline Gardiner missed them most acutely. She had maintained correspondence with Elizabeth and heard all about the dinner at Netherfield, the house hunting and her struggles to accustom herself to being engaged. On a rare Tuesday, Mr. Gardiner returned home for luncheon to find his wife reading the latest missive from Hertfordshire and laughing out loud.

"What has Fanny done now?"

"No, not Fanny. It appears Mr. Darcy was a little high-handed with Elizabeth and she served him a taste of 'careful what you wish for' or in his case, demand."

Mr. Gardiner placed his napkin on his lap and helped himself to part of the meat pie. His brows furrowed. "He isn't mistreating her, is he? I won't let any of my nieces marry a brute."

"No, no! Nothing like that. He just demanded to be present when Charlotte Lucas, now Collins, visited recently. Elizabeth writes that she made sure to directly ask Mr. Darcy his opinion on every subject the ladies discussed. By the time they began the topic of lace, she says the gentleman suddenly remembered a promise he made to Bingley!"

The two Gardiners laughed heartily at the predicament and tears began to form in Mrs. Gardiner's eyes. She inhaled a few deep breaths so she could continue her letter. Mr. Gardiner, having spent most of the morning working hard on receiving the first of his vessels this quarter, wasted no time in finishing his first portion of meat pie and helping himself to another.

"Oh dear. She writes that not much has progressed for Jane. I agree with her that Jane's serene manners might not serve to encourage Mr. Bingley."

Mr. Gardiner held his fork for a moment in thought, then took the bite. After swallowing, he wiped his mouth with his napkin. "I confess I don't think too much of that Bingley fellow. He doesn't appear to be a steady sort. Can't say I see him as a suitable match for our Jane."

"Be that as it may, with Lydia's situation, the girls would suffer if he should break off the courtship."

Mr. Gardiner nodded and sighed. He checked his pocket watch and shook his head. He needed to return to the warehouses before too long. Silently he prayed his oldest daughter, Amelia, would slow her growth. Though he felt strongly for his nieces, he knew when his own daughter's time came, it would be a hundred times worse.

"What does Elizabeth say about their plans? Are they to marry from Hertfordshire?"

Mrs. Gardiner shook her head. "No, their plans

are not yet set, and it looks like she has received some guidance from Lady Matlock. They are planning to see Fanny settled and then return to London for presentation to society before celebrating Easter in Derbyshire at Matlock."

"What a brave new world our Lizzie has fallen into." Mr. Gardiner reached over for his wife's hand and brought it to his lips for a kiss. Mrs. Gardiner looked up at her husband and blushed, while her other hand reached down to touch her stomach. She couldn't be sure, but the signs were that a fifth Gardiner child was on its merry way to the world. "Perhaps after they marry we will have a chance to visit Lambton."

"I fear we may have to wait until winter or next spring, Husband." Mrs. Gardiner raised her glass of wine to take a drink.

"Is it? Is it certain?" he asked hopefully.

She shook her head. "Not yet, but soon."

Mr. Gardiner smiled and rose from the table. "You are as beautiful as the day we met, Madeline." Leaving his wife to blush even more, Edward Gardiner felt light as he headed back to his dusty warehouses and the crates of goods he still needed to see dispersed throughout the country.

Chapter Five

"**M**ama! Please, be reasonable! The cottage is ready," Elizabeth Bennet pleaded with her mother for what felt like the hundredth time in a week.

"You don't understand these things, Lizzie. You've yet to run your own household. Yes, a few more days, perhaps a week and the final details attended to, and Lydia will . . . "

Her mother continued to fritter on, but Elizabeth had stopped listening as frustration began throbbing in her ears. Her heart raced, and she focused on taking a few calming breaths. For three weeks Elizabeth's mother had dragged her feet, and now that she had been invited to Matlock for the Easter holiday next month, she desperately wanted to return to London to prepare her trousseau. Her future aunt, the Countess Matlock, had made it plainly clear that this holiday would begin her transformation from a small country squire's daughter to the illustrious Mrs. Darcy.

". . . and Kitty will need new furnishings as the castoffs that are currently in the home are below our station--"

"What station? You are a widow with five

unmarried daughters."

"Tsk, tsk, you will soon be married to Mr. Darcy and he wouldn't wish his mother-in-law to live in abject poverty. No, no, we will need finer linens and must commission a new set of silver." Mrs. Bennet continued to chatter away about the expenses she planned to incur as Mr. Darcy's mother-in-law.

The frustration Elizabeth felt turned to boiling rage. She stood up from her seat and glared at her mother. Not trusting her mouth to say anything remotely gentle, she simply scowled and donned her spencer. She left her mother in the parlor with Jane and Lydia. Elizabeth's feet carried her in the direction of Netherfield, away from town, without a conscious thought on her part.

A carriage traveling much too fast for the roads hurtled past her, and Elizabeth stepped well out of the way. Instead of continuing along the road, she opted for a detour into the woods she now knew very well since moving to her Aunt Phillips' home. Soon, she arrived in a peaceful glen and was cheered to see winter's thaw had set upon the countryside. A babbling brook soothed her frayed nerves, and Elizabeth found a fallen log to serve as her bench. Turning her face up to the sunlight pouring between the still-bare tree branches just beginning to bud, she felt her anger and frustration also melt away.

"Lizzie?"

Elizabeth sighed as she recognized her sister Kitty's voice. "Over here," she called out, reluctant to cede her peaceful moment. When she looked down and opened her eyes, she stifled a laugh at the sight of poor Kitty fighting every low-lying tree branch determined to snag her cloak. Brushing her hands of the small bits of bark stuck to her palms, Elizabeth stood and modestly brushed the seat of her skirt. She met Kitty halfway and pulled the branches aside to allow her easier passage.

"Ugh, the woods are so disagreeable!" Kitty fumed as she pulled twigs from her person. "I don't know how you manage."

"I stick to the path." Elizabeth laughed as Kitty frowned.

"You need to come back. A woman named Lady Catherine de Bourgh has just arrived. It doesn't appear to be a cordial call." Elizabeth immediately hastened back through the woods without a thought as to how Kitty was keeping up. She stomped through mud, caring not as the twigs and branches brushed her face and bonnet. By the time she reached the outskirts of her aunt's yard, she was out of breath. Doubled over and panting, Elizabeth took a moment to collect herself as she could already hear raised voices inside. Before she could enter, Kitty caught up, also out of breath.

"Go to the stables and send someone to Netherfield. Tell them to fetch Mr. Darcy." Kitty nodded and hurried off while Elizabeth did her best to fix her appearance. When she heard her mother howl, Elizabeth knew she could wait no longer and rushed to the door.

The scene in the parlor was as she expected. Her sisters and mother cowered in one corner with Lady Catherine standing in the doorway banging her blasted walking stick and spewing her vitriol. "I cannot accept that you are incapable of keeping even the slightest knowledge of your daughter's whereabouts. Now tell me this instant where I can find that harlot!"

With a serene smile, Elizabeth marched forward and purposely bumped into Lady Catherine to enter the room. "Begging your pardon, whatever brings you to our home, Lady Catherine?" Elizabeth turned around to face her adversary, standing firmly between her family and the woman.

"I have come to appeal to your better senses. I have heard all about the mussed up engagement of your sister and that lazy, no good Wickham. Surely you do not wish to see the Darcy name pulled down to the lowly status of the beastly Bennets."

Elizabeth crossed her arms and stared at the old woman trying her best to command a regal posture. After a moment, Elizabeth burst out laughing. "You are the worst manipulator of wills I've ever seen. Even if I could be plied upon to abandon Mr. Darcy for the good of his name, I would never be convinced by such a mean spirit as you, milady." Elizabeth added the courtesy with a mocking voice.

"This is not to be borne! Darcy will marry my daughter. You are merely a dalliance in a long line of distractions." Lady Catherine waved her hand to emphasize the trifling nature of her nephew's attentions.

The insinuation of Darcy's earlier interests stung Elizabeth's heart, but she ignored the well-placed arrow for the moment. She wasn't about to give Lady Catherine the satisfaction. "Lady Catherine, you are not welcome in my home or any other place I may be visiting. You will leave at once," Elizabeth commanded, standing to her full height, which was a full two inches greater than the woman's from Kent. After giving the woman a look of disgust, Elizabeth turned her back to look at her frightened mother and sisters.

"Ho, ho, not so quickly. I will have my say. Darcy is a most ancient family, and what of Bennet?" Lady Catherine demanded as she grabbed Elizabeth's shoulder to turn her back around.

"If you direct your carriage to the church, you'll find eight generations of Bennets entombed there," Elizabeth said, flatly. She brushed the lady's hand off her shoulder and stared coldly at her sneering face.

"But what of your pedigree? Your stature? Your family could not even manage to keep that leaky old estate in your family name. I heard your father plundered the coffers; what a lout he must have been. I'm sure your mother is quite happy to be free." Lady Catherine made a small, satisfied smile as Elizabeth's face turned beet red, and her mother gasped loudly.

Elizabeth inhaled deeply through her nose and marched forward to stand nose to nose with Lady Catherine. "Do not tempt me, madam, to further embarrass you by having you thrown out of this house."

"You wouldn't dare!"

"Leave! We don't wish to look at your ugly cow face any longer!" Lydia called out from the corner where she was perfectly protected by her mother.

"Why you little. . . ." Lady Catherine lurched forward trying to get past Elizabeth, but the older woman's frailer frame wasn't a match for Elizabeth's physique. With her legs firmly planted on the floor, Elizabeth held her ground as Lady Catherine crashed into her and stumbled back. Shocked, the older woman began to fall backwards, and Elizabeth panicked and reached out to grab her. Steadying the older woman as best she could, Elizabeth was perturbed, but not surprised, when Lady Catherine slapped her hands away and gained her balance.

"Get away from me! You shall not touch my person!" she bellowed for all to hear. Kitty entered from the outside in time to see the stand off between her sister and the lady, but she lost her voice as the older woman began banging the floor with her cane once more. Elizabeth clutched her skirts in one hand to maintain her temper and held her position so that the only place for Lady Catherine to go was between the two Bennet sisters, towards the front door.

Lady Catherine began to berate Elizabeth once more at the unseemly departure. "I know how to deal with you. Just you watch. Before I'm through, you'll be turned away from every respectable household in the country. I shall never forget this!" she hissed. With an exaggerated limp, Lady Catherine made her way to the door where Kitty took a step back to give the peeress plenty of room to make her exit. Once the old thorn was outside, Elizabeth couldn't help but laugh, and Kitty soon joined with her.

"Elizabeth Bennet, do you have any idea what you've done? You've ruined us all, putting your hands on a peer! Oohhh, the constable will come and carry you away!" Mrs. Bennet began yelling most cruelly to her daughter, causing Elizabeth to turn around.

"No, Mama, he will not. Lady Catherine is Mr. Darcy's aunt."

Mrs. Bennet wailed even louder. "We're ruined! He'll abandon you now! He'll never marry you now that you've assaulted his aunt!"

"Mama! Please, Mr. Darcy will not press charges. Nor will he give me up. This is not the first time that lady has tried to intervene."

For a moment, Mrs. Bennet blinked her eyes and processed the information her second eldest daughter imparted. Then she shook her head and began to wail again.

"Shhh, Mama. It will all be fine. Lydia? Help me take her upstairs?" Jane pleaded with her younger sister, who scoffed in response. Carefully the two girls guided their mother, who was crying and carrying on, up the stairs. Elizabeth found the pressure in her head had quickly returned.

Once more she exited the house, only to see a horse in the far distance. Without caring, Elizabeth took off in a run toward the horse. Mr. Darcy slowed his pace as he could make out Elizabeth running towards him. He jumped off Poseidon and was ready when the young woman simply collapsed into his arms. Clasping her tightly, he whispered to her. "Shhh, you're safe now. I'm truly sorry for whatever my aunt has caused."

Elizabeth leaned back and wiped her eyes, sniffling in an attempt to regain her senses. "She tried to attack Lydia and ran into me and nearly fell to the ground, but I held onto her. I fear she is most displeased."

Darcy shook his head and ignored Poseidon's signs of aggravation at standing still. "She struck you?"

"No, no," Elizabeth made a final wipe at her eyes. "She was pure evil. She spoke against my father. Lydia called her a cow and when she lunged forward, I blocked her way, nearly knocking her down. I'm so sorry, William."

"I'm sure nothing but her pride was injured."

Elizabeth tucked her head back to his chest and sighed. "How did you arrive so quickly? Kitty just sent the messenger."

Darcy grimaced. "I had already been on my way for our daily visit. If I had but left a little earlier, I might have saved you from my aunt's wrath."

Elizabeth shook her head. "No, my dear, if you had been present, I believe she would have behaved ten times worse." For a moment, Elizabeth simply enjoyed the comfort of his arms before she leaned back to address a new subject. "William, can we leave for London, tomorrow?"

"Absolutely, my darling. We'll leave at first light."

꽃 꽃 꽃 꽃 꽃 꽃 꽃 꽃 꽃

The Darcy carriage creaked and groaned on a surprisingly warm March morning with Darcy, Elizabeth, Kitty and the maid Becky inside on their way to London. Jane remained behind since Bingley would stay at Netherfield until the full season began. With Lydia becoming more and more irritable each day, Elizabeth happily invited Kitty to come with her to London with promises to take to her to many social events in the interest of character inspiration for her writing pursuits.

Jane Bennet looked out the window not one hour after her sisters had left to see Mr. Bingley driving up in a curricle. Smiling, she hurried to the peering glass in the hallway to check her appearance, then found a seat in the parlor to await Mr. Bingley's arrival. It was lucky indeed that her mother and Lydia had just left for Meryton for yet another trip to find provisions for the cottage. As Mr. Bingley entered the parlor, he bowed, and Jane rose to curtsy.

"Miss Bennet, I wondered, that is, would you care to take a ride this morning?" Jane blushed and nodded affirmatively. She donned a spencer and her bonnet, and butterflies began to flutter in her stomach. Although her courtship with Mr. Bingley hadn't been so quick as Elizabeth's with Mr. Darcy, Jane had hopes that perhaps today he planned to make their understanding permanent.

The curricle was a much smoother ride than Jane had anticipated as Charles Bingley expertly guided the two ponies around the road through Meryton. Jane waved to friends and to her mother and Lydia as they happened to be outside the butcher shop. Mrs. Bennet squealed and waved her handkerchief in response, causing Jane to blush even more, but wear a broad smile. As soon as they steered out of town, Bingley urged the ponies faster and faster, and the speed began to make Jane's stomach lurch. As they careened around a corner and Jane could feel the wheel on her side lift off the ground, she let out a scream. "Please, Charles, slow down! This is much too fast."

"It's supposed to go this fast!" he laughed and spurred the ponies faster. Jane grasped one hand onto her bonnet to keep it in place and squeezed her eyes shut. She couldn't watch and just knew the curricle was going to crash. As they came to another turn, Mr. Bingley's hip slid into hers as his side of the curricle came up.

"I demand that you stop this at once, Charles Bingley!" Jane shouted. The uncharacteristic demanding tone shocked Charles into calming the ponies, but it was a good quarter mile before the curricle slowed to a stop. As soon as the wheels came to a halt, Jane Bennet shoved herself away from Mr. Bingley and helped herself down.

"Jane! Please, Miss Bennet!" Jane began to walk back towards town, feeling so very cross with herself for imagining that the sweet man she met at the assembly all those months ago had returned. Instead, here was the Mr. Bingley she became acquainted with in London, a man with a quick smile, congenial attitude, and complete disregard for the serious things in life. She continued to walk, but already the rocks on the road were making her slippered feet ache.

"Please, Miss Bennet. You must stop. I will drive you back."

"Not in that, you won't. You nearly killed us both!" she shouted back.

Charles struggled to keep control of the curricle and keep the ponies as slow as the pace of Miss Bennet's walking. Finally he stopped the curricle altogether and jumped down. He rushed around to the front of the ponies to head Miss Bennet off on the right side. At first she tried to sidestep him, but he held out his arms, and she finally stopped and crossed her arms.

"I never meant to hurt you, Jane. I drive this fast all the time on these roads; it's a complete rush, I tell you." Still she frowned at him, and Bingley took off his hat in contrition. "I had hoped to give you a small thrill, a little excitement since we've both been cooped up in parlors and drawing rooms." He looked at the ground in shame.

Jane couldn't stay angry with him. "Do you

promise to slow down? It would be very pleasant to ride and have some conversation." She gave him a small smile as he looked up at her. He reached for her hand and kissed the top.

"I solemnly promise. I'll even give you the reins and let you drive." Jane's eyes lit up when he offered to let her drive. Carefully, he helped her back into the curricle, and they began the trip back to town, this time at a quarter of the speed they had left town. Jane relished controlling the ponies and felt herself sitting taller and more elevated in the leather bench seat of the equipage. "Can you imagine spending our Saturday afternoons riding in London just so?" Bingley began a conversation about their potential future lives. Jane twisted her mouth into a line of disapproval.

"Perhaps we would spend our afternoons riding just so here in Hertfordshire? You do plan to purchase Netherfield, do you not?"

"To be honest, my plans are not yet set. That is, purchasing an estate was my father's dream, and while I leased the property to learn more about owning an estate, I cannot say that it's a dream of mine. I find London suits my needs much more closely."

A small bump in the road jostled Jane, and Charles reached over to steady her hands. The touch was novel, but Jane didn't find it made her heart flutter as it had before. Her disappointment in losing what she counted as her future—raising her family amongst families she had known her whole life—had darkened her mood. Loving Bingley and becoming his wife looked to be the surest way to find herself lost in the London crowd. Faced suddenly with a new prospect, Jane didn't know what she thought about such a dramatically different future from what she had seen for herself.

As the curricle came back into sight of Meryton, Jane offered the reins back to Charles and answered his other queries with pleasant conversation. They arrived at her aunt's home just as her mother and Lydia were returning, and Jane gave a meek farewell to Mr. Bingley before allowing her mother to shower him with her effusive compliments.

Chapter Six

The strength and duration of Madeline Gardiner's hugs made Elizabeth and Kitty Bennet blush. Her home bereft of the cheer the young women brought to its walls had been of too long an endurance, and the girls' aunt had no qualms about showing how much she desired their company.

"How was the journey? I'm certain you are positively worn out, even if Mr. Darcy's carriage is well-sprung."

Elizabeth and Kitty shared a look. The frazzled fussing made both girls raise an eyebrow and giggle. Their aunt convincingly mimicked their own mother only during a certain condition.

"We are well. Mr. Darcy made sure we stopped at many inns along the way to stretch and rest. I think the trip was longer by two hours on account of his fastidious care!" Elizabeth related to her aunt.

"All the same, there is water on boil so you each may take a bath. Dinner will be served in just a few hours if you wish to go upstairs and rest. Kitty will stay in the smaller room, and Mary will move over to room with you, Elizabeth. We expect her any moment now from Matlock House."

As Elizabeth began to take the stairs, she paused and looked back down at her aunt. "Mary wasn't visiting at Darcy House with Miss Darcy?"

Aunt Gardiner shook her head. "Both girls were collected by Lady Matlock and have been enjoying the last few weeks with her." Placing her hands together, Madeline Gardiner made her way back towards the kitchen, mumbling giddily to herself that tonight her girls would all be together again.

Kitty and Elizabeth both paused on the landing before separating to their individual rooms. Elizabeth noticed Kitty's hesitation and gave her younger sister a warm smile.

"It shall always be this way for me, won't it? Shuffled back and forth to relatives until I marry . . .," Kitty said.

"I know it's difficult. But only the first time," Elizabeth replied.

Kitty took a deep breath and opened the door to her room. Charming green curtains hung on the small window of the far wall. There was a single bed and bureau furnishing the room. "Back in Meryton, I could pretend this was all just temporary."

"He would be very proud of you, Kitty. You've matured and grown. I'm sorry he was not--not so considerate of you and Lydia when he was here," Elizabeth said softly, wincing as she admitted her late father's faults. She turned quickly into the room she would now share with Mary, leaving Kitty to settle in on her own. Elizabeth curled up on the familiar bed she had slept in for every visit to London since she was fourteen. The fatigue from her stress and travels weighed heavily on her body. After a few salty tears slid down her cheeks, Elizabeth closed her eyes and fell asleep.

Her slumber didn't last long, for less than an hour later, Mary Bennet opened the door to their shared bedroom, and Elizabeth popped up from the bed with the fatigue of her recent tears making her eyes sting. She rubbed them and yawned.

"Forgive me; I wasn't made aware you were sleeping," Mary offered. Elizabeth immediately noticed something different in the way her sister carried herself. There wasn't Mary the Mouse in front of her looking down at her feet as she apologized, but a confident young woman with a sincere look of concern on her face.

Elizabeth rose from the bed and greeted Mary with a warm hug.

"Was it so very awful?" the younger Bennet sister asked.

Elizabeth walked over to the looking glass and used the cool water in the basin to refresh her face. She shivered at the temperature and dried her cheeks with the towel. "You cannot possibly fathom! From disastrous dinners to Mama trying to make William spend more money at every turn, I was constantly appalled at our family's behavior! Were we really so awful before?"

Mary gave Elizabeth a twisted smile. "So it's William, now?"

Both sisters enjoyed a giggle. "Yes, when we are in private, we call each other by our Christian names. I admit that for some time, that's what I've called him in my thoughts."

The door opened to their room and a more familiar version of the lively Kitty appeared. "There's an officer downstairs! A large, tall man with the handsomest brown eyes! He's to dine with us!" She left the door, then reappeared briefly. "And Mr. Darcy is here!"

Elizabeth furrowed her brow, then smiled. "It must be Colonel Fitzwilliam, Mr. Darcy's cousin." Elizabeth walked past Mary to follow Kitty out of the room, but didn't miss the flushed color spreading from her younger sister's cheeks and down her neck. Elizabeth made a mental note to acquaint Mary with her and Jane's midnight chats tonight to get to the bottom of what all her visit at Matlock House entailed.

Dinner in the Gardiner home was far more pleasant than any Darcy and Elizabeth had enjoyed in Hertfordshire. Darcy didn't just bring his cousin, but also his younger sister, Georgiana, and she and Kitty were getting on famously down at the end of the table closest to Mrs. Gardiner. Elizabeth felt hopeful to see the two young women converse with such high spirits. Across from her, she kept a watchful eye on Mary, sitting next to the Colonel, and couldn't help sharing a slightly amused look with her uncle as she noticed Mary blush again. With a small smile, Elizabeth turned her attention back to her plate and took another bite of candied carrots.

"Are you very fond of carrots?" Mr. Darcy interrupted her thoughts.

Elizabeth compared her plate where her carrots were nearly gone and Mr. Darcy's plate that had no trace of carrots ever being there. "They are a particular favorite of mine. But you appear to not enjoy them, sir?"

"Indeed, I find myself much more pleased to leave the orange roots for those they are intended for." He paused for a moment and then shared the answer with her as if he was releasing state secrets. "Rabbits."

Elizabeth couldn't resist a good tease and turned her face to her fiance. She scrunched her nose up and down in a most impressive imitation of a bunny. "We heartily thank you, sir."

Darcy laughed and the novelty of the sound made the Colonel and Mary stop their conversation to look at the couple across from them.

"I say, Darce, heaven shines on a man whose wife can make him laugh."

"Hear, hear!" Mr. Gardiner answered and raised his glass in toast.

Darcy wiped his mouth with his napkin to try to hide his continued jubilation. He reflected that in the future, he should be very mindful to not take a drink or mouthful of food when he was baiting the future Mrs. Darcy.

"Thank you, Colonel. But I assure you, it wasn't my intention to only make Mr. Darcy laugh, but also not take offense at his calling me a rabbit."

"Darcy! Surely not! From what I hear, Miss Elizabeth is a most ferocious knight, able to slay dragons!"

Elizabeth rolled her eyes but it was her sister Kitty who jumped in to take the Colonel's bait. "What dragon? Lizzie doesn't slay dragons. That's absurd!"

"Au contraire, Miss Kitty, I heard a report that she bested my Aunt Catherine, and if ever there were a dragon, it is she." The whole table erupted in laughter as all present had been privy to some version of the truth that caused Darcy and Elizabeth to finally quit Hertfordshire. "I believe my mother plans to erect a statue to you in her garden: Elizabeth the Brave with a foot on Catherine the Coward."

"Richard, that's taking it a bit too far." Darcy responded.

"I apologize, Colonel, but I fear that I side with Mr. Darcy. I am not proud of my actions towards your aunt, and I would hate to be the cause for a rift in the family." Elizabeth found her hunger had simply slipped away as she was reminded about the potential consequences of her actions.

The Colonel waved his hand. "If I have offended, then I apologize, but I think you will find that more people in London are apt to shake your hand, Miss Elizabeth, than chastise you over standing up to Lady Catherine for the second time. Remind me to never get on your bad side, eh?"

"Being on my good side or bad side is entirely up to you, sir." Elizabeth raised an eyebrow and flicked her eyes to her sister Mary and back again.

"Ho, ho! I concede, Elizabeth the Brave; this soldier will be on his best behavior."

Darcy frowned, not enjoying the familiarity of conversation passing between his cousin and Elizabeth. He cleared his throat and addressed Mr. Gardiner. "I brought a box of cigars from my private collection if you would like to partake?"

Mrs. Gardiner acknowledged that dinner was over and began to rise from the table, causing the three men to also rise. "Ladies, shall we retire to the drawing room? I think we have certain plans to discuss," she said as she made sure to lightly brush her husband's hand as she walked by Mr. Gardiner standing proudly at the head of the table. The Bennet sisters and Georgiana stood and followed the older woman's lead, with Georgiana making sure to smile and nod to her brother as a sign that she was quite comfortable.

"Alright, gentlemen, since you are providing the smoke, I shall provide the cognac."

Mr. Gardiner pulled down his waistcoat that continually bothered him when he sat or stood and escorted the two young men to his study. Darcy paused for a moment upon entering the room, his eyes settled on the window seat where he had finally managed to win Elizabeth's heart with a game of chess.

"Don't look now, but we've lost the love-sick Darcy again, I'm afraid." The Colonel continued to hold out the glass to his cousin as he had done so for a few moments. Darcy shook his head and shrugged his shoulders, taking the proffered glass and finding a seat closest to the door.

"Ah, leave be, Colonel. It is said those who tease loudest are likely to suffer a similar affliction all too soon themselves."

Richard shifted his weight uncomfortably from foot to foot and moved to inspect a great naval battle depicted on the far wall of the Gardiner study. "Were you a Navy man, Mr. Gardiner?" Richard asked, noting the amazing detail of the two warships firing upon one another.

"Sadly, no. But I always wished to be! Unfortunately, I'm horrifically land-legged. Couldn't even stomach a proper boat rowing with Madeline back when we were courting."

"Does Miss Elizabeth enjoy the water?" Darcy asked.

"I think that might best be a question for you to

ask of her, a nice neutral subject for a sitting room under observation of others." Mr. Gardiner touched his nose with his forefinger.

"Yeah, Darce, what the devil made you come back to London so early? A good country ramble with your intended seems far too great an inducement to rush back to the prying harpies of society. It couldn't have been that bad, could it?"

"Ugh, the vulgarities of Mrs. Bennet are beyond what you can imagine, Cousin. Forgive me, Mr. Gardiner; she is your sister."

"No, no, Son, you're perfectly free to share your burdens here. I'm much acquainted with both of my sisters and hold no delusions where their manners are concerned."

Darcy nodded and continued his tales of absurdity and outright fleecing between the behavior of Caroline Bingley and Mrs. Bennet. It wasn't long before all three men in the study were howling with laughter.

In the drawing room, the ladies were of a decidedly different bent. As Kitty was asked to pour the tea in her first official practice of London living, Mrs. Gardiner started the conversation about the upcoming plans to visit her home county of Derbyshire.

"It is such a lovely place, with rolling hills and stunning pastures. There is a particular shade of green that I confess I miss with all my heart." Mrs. Gardiner reminisced and carefully stirred her tea. She tried to keep her emotions under good regulation, but a wave of homesickness flooded her heightened senses, and her eyes began to mist over. Not wishing to make the girls uncomfortable, she looked up at the ceiling for a moment and then back down with a warm smile back in place.

"I am so happy to hear we share a home county! Our home is my favorite place in all of England. Just wait until we can walk the gardens, Elizabeth, and I can't wait to see you plan your roses," Georgiana exclaimed.

Elizabeth coughed on her tea, but steadied herself. "Pardon me, but my roses?"

Georgiana nodded most enthusiastically. "Yes, all of the Mistresses of Pemberley plan their own rose gardens. I spend more time in my mother's, but I do also like Great-Grandmother Darcy's circular path of increasingly deeper shades of pink."

"There is more than one rose garden at your home?" Kitty asked.

Georgiana looked at the three Bennet sisters and realized she had committed a faux pas. She hadn't meant to emphasize the difference in their stations, and her brother had warned her of just that very thing.

Mrs. Gardiner patted Elizabeth's hand and offered her a warm smile. "How foolish of us to make all of these plans about your Easter trip! Dash over to your uncle's study, and see if the gentlemen are finished with their smoke, would you, dear?"

Elizabeth agreed silently and placed her teacup and saucer on the table to her left.

She calmly exited the room but her mind was racing. She was expected to plan a garden? A garden that would stand as a testament to her abilities for generations to come? Just how much responsibility had she taken on without proper consideration? The expanse of Pemberley grew by epic proportions in her mind as she considered just how large an estate must be to have multiple rose gardens. As she neared the door, she took a few moments to gather her wits when she could hear Mr. Darcy's voice loudly from inside.

"And she wanted a second silver serving set just to be prepared should the Earl and Countess come to call and the first one be tarnished! I tell you, if we hadn't escaped, I might have just told the woman she could live at Pemberley to stop all of the shopping excursions!"

Elizabeth's cheeks burned as she could hear her uncle and Richard laugh along with her fiance at the silliness of her mother. Incensed, her loyalty immediately flew to her family. Elizabeth felt very indignant that Mr. Darcy had no right, no right whatsoever, to make fun of her mother. Didn't he realize that as a daughter of a solicitor, a visit from his aunt and uncle would very likely be the highlight of her life as a widow? How could he be so cruel?

Biting her lip, Elizabeth set her features to channel the serenity of her older sister, Jane, as she knocked on the door. With no response, she knocked once more, more purposely, and her small knuckles finally made a pert, hollow sound the men inside could hear. The laughter immediately stopped and the door swung open to show her uncle's perspiring and ruddy face.

"Aunt wished for me to see if you gentlemen would care to join us as we are discussing the upcoming trip to Matlock." Elizabeth curtsied and turned on her heel without waiting for a response.

"Oh, dear." Mr. Gardiner said, and he quickly turned around to look at the man he largely considered to be his future son-in-law, if not in name, then at least in spirit. "I do believe we are about to enter the lion's den, my lads."

"I'd say we should all guard our loins, but I think only Darcy here needs to take that advice."

"The cavalry man being cavalier, how novel," Darcy spouted, dryly. In actuality, his heart thumped wildly against his chest, and his stomach felt unsettled. How much of his unburdening had Elizabeth heard? His palms slick with cold sweat, he downed the last of his drink and exited the room as a man ready to face the music.

Instinct told him to take a detour to the sitting room by way of the dining room. Handsomely rewarded, Elizabeth stood on the opposite side of the room with her back to him. He cleared his throat but she didn't turn.

"I believe I owe you an apology. What you heard—"

"Was not your honest opinion? Was not true? Pray tell me, which is it?" She stood as a statue for a moment awaiting his response. Behind her, Mr. Darcy simply opened and closed his mouth a few times, confounded with finding the right words to say.

She turned around with angry tears poised to fall. Darcy was stricken, and as she looked at his face, pale with concern, she blinked her eyes a few times and the deluge released. Within moments of closing her eyes to try to stem the flow of tears, she felt once again the comfort of being in his arms.

"Elizabeth, sweet Elizabeth," he whispered. Registering his voice, she shoved him away.

"No, sir! You are not permitted to embrace me

and make me forget my feelings."

"I make you forget your anger when I hold you?" he asked, trying to diminish her distress with distraction.

"That is not the salient point, sir. What I meant is you may not come walking into this room--"

"This room in particular? I had no idea I was banned from the dining room." Darcy sniffed as he looked around, pretending to be offended.

"Again, you are twisting my words!"

"I've learned from the best, my little rabbit." And in a rare show of flirtation, Fitzwilliam Reginald George Darcy wrinkled his nose up and down, and his Elizabeth laughed. After a few moments of listening to her tinkling laughter and resisting the temptation to whisk her off her adorable feet, Darcy remained patient. "I am most truly and humbly sorry."

Elizabeth sighed and wrapped her arms around her intended to embrace him for once. Her hands could barely meet around the back of his coat, and taking a deep breath, she slightly squeezed. The feeling was still a shock to Darcy. He froze, unsure of what advances she would welcome from him. Eventually, he relaxed and embraced her back with gentle pressure. All too soon, she pulled away.

"Just because you have not heard the worst of my words about your aunt, does not mean I did not utter them. We both have relations that . . ."

"That we would wish to banish to the Colonies?"

Elizabeth shook her head.

"Not invite to dinner?"

Biting her lip, Elizabeth nodded. Catching Mr. Darcy's eyes, she released her grim expression and couldn't help but smile at the dashing man before her.

Lifting her hand and pressing his lips against the back of it, he gave her a smile that showed off his dimples. "Madam, if we can endeavor to resolve our differences in such a manner once we are married, then I prognosticate a truly happy union, indeed."

Elizabeth's heart fluttered at his mention of their future married state as she allowed him to escort her back to the sitting room for further discussion of their trip.

A small voice continued to complain in the back of her mind with certainty that she could never live up to the expectations of being Mrs. Darcy of Pemberley. These whispers nagged her from the dark corners of her insecurity. But for a night, she made an effort to banish those thoughts for another time and resolved to end at least one dinner party with Mr. Darcy on a happy note.

Chapter Seven

Bleary-eyed, Fitzwilliam Darcy finished his tenth letter for the morning before setting his pen down and rubbing his face with the palm of his hand. A yawn escaped from his mouth as the door to his study was knocked upon. "Enter." He leaned back in his chair as his sister came into the room, clearly ebullient from a well-rested night. Darcy, meanwhile, had suffered through two weeks of early rising to finish his work before a reasonable hour in order to pay a call on the Gardiner residence and then return or stay for dinner and an evening's entertainment.

"Good morning, William. It's quite warm out today, and I've just received a note back from Mary. We are in agreement for a picnic this afternoon with the Miss Bennets in Hyde Park." Georgiana smiled brightly and made a tiny clapping motion with her hands.

"I am happy to hear the plans are set. Have you visited the kitchens to discuss this with Mrs. Palmer?"

Georgiana's smile faded. "Er, no. Would not Mrs. Kensington take care of the details?"

"To be sure, she is most capable of planning a small picnic, but I think it best for you to undertake this excursion. Good practice for your own future and all that." A small pout began to quiver on his sister's lip, and Darcy laughed. "None of that false fear, if you please. Now off with you, I am too exhausted to trifle with any silliness you have planned to play at this morning."

Making a face at her much older brother, Georgiana Darcy curtsied and exited her brother's study. This new workload he was placing on her shoulders was most vexing, and she was beginning to find truth in what her brother and cousin had always told her. There was truly no fun in growing up.

Giving his arms a stretch, Darcy looked once more over his correspondence before growling at a pile of at least another fifteen letters that all required his reply. He glanced at the clock on the mantle and resolved to respond to five more before he had to leave to meet with his solicitor. Mending his pen and opening a new bottle of ink, the Master of Pemberley and other properties set back to work.

Across the city on Gracechurch Street, Elizabeth Bennet was happy to entertain her younger cousins with tales of the daring Bennet sisters in Hertfordshire so many years ago. After telling of the time she and Jane triumphed over the mean Lucas' boys by disguising a rather deep mud puddle with well-placed sticks and foliage, young Master Gardiner only wondered one thing.

"Did your Papa whip you?" he asked, eyes wide. Since being warned of such a fate by his own father last week for running in the hall and knocking into Mother, Peter Gardiner was very keen to know more about what did and did not constitute a whipping offense.

Shocked at the mention of her father, Elizabeth took a beat to swallow and considered her answer. Her father had never raised a hand to any of his daughters. She shook her head and gave her young cousins a weak smile.

"My papa would have! He does not like it when you break the rules."

"Only when breaking the rules can hurt another, Peter. Now you two are late for your lessons, and Nanny is waiting." Mrs. Gardiner appeared with a bouquet of lovely daffodils in her arms and swooshed into the room to replace the wilted flowers hanging limply in a vase positioned in the main window. Her two children scurried up the stairs without argument. "I hope they didn't distress you much."

"Not at all. I was happy to give Nanny Pierce a break." Elizabeth rose to take over the flower arranging duties from her aunt. Mrs. Gardiner collapsed into a chair and fanned her face. Smirking, Elizabeth turned away from observing her aunt and stood on her tiptoes to see higher over the vase to the street beyond. The hustle and bustle of the street was too chaotic for her to make out very much, but a strange man standing on the far street corner gave her pause. He wasn't moving, and he was too far for Elizabeth to see the details of his face, heavily shrouded by his hat. Shrugging, she reasoned he must be waiting to deliver a message or have other such business to conduct.

Seeing her aunt still in distress, Elizabeth picked up the footstool and moved it closer to her aunt's feet, helping her to prop them up. "I could have called a maid," the older woman scolded Elizabeth, who just responded with a wan smile.

"I carefully balanced the needs of my dearest relation with the convenience of waiting for a servant and ultimately concluded that I could indeed deign to move a mighty footstool." The two women shared a laugh, and Elizabeth took a seat near her aunt. Mrs. Gardiner couldn't help herself and absently rubbed the small, growing bump in her midsection. Noticing her niece eyeing her hands' movements, Madeline Gardiner looked down and blushed.

"Forgive me; I suppose the surprise your uncle and I planned to share at dinner tonight is ruined."

Elizabeth shook her head. "We all knew you were expecting weeks ago." Madeline Gardiner's mouth dropped in shock.

"Was I so very transparent?"

Again, Elizabeth laughed and shook her head. "No, but I've practically spent half a year here every year since I've been out. I've witnessed all of your symptoms for all four of the children."

Wincing slightly, Mrs. Gardiner adjusted her posture to stop the aches and pains of her body accommodating itself to the life growing inside. "I don't recall feeling so tired and worn with the other four. Oooh."

Elizabeth worried as her aunt's face paled, and she quickly stood up. "I will send for the doctor. And Uncle."

"You will do no such thing! Sit back down!" Her aunt continued to take a few breaths through her nose and then suddenly smiled. "This is nothing but normal. I'm sorry you had to witness my imposition."

Slowly, Elizabeth returned to her chair and arched her eyebrows. "Are you sure I shouldn't tell

Uncle?"

"I simply tried to do a little too much this morning, and my body is reminding me to slow down. Now, forget me for a moment. Let's talk about you while we have the privacy. Do you have any questions about your future with Mr. Darcy?" Elizabeth reddened and looked away. Mrs. Gardiner reached over to pat her hands. "It's perfectly safe, dear. Women do talk about these things, and you are very soon to be married. I've watched him with you, and I don't think you have anything to fear in that corner."

Elizabeth's head shot up. "Fear? Why ever should I fear him?"

Madeline Gardiner took a deep breath and sighed. "There are some wives who do not learn until it's too late their husband is a brute and takes his own pleasure with or without regard to their wives' wishes."

Elizabeth's mouth dropped in horror, and Mrs. Gardiner nodded her head to confirm that what she was thinking was indeed the nightmare her aunt was trying to describe.

"It's an ugly business, that. And unless a woman has a father or brother to step in . . . well, you have nothing to worry about." Mrs. Gardiner attempted a wane smile in support.

Leaving Elizabeth stunned in her chair, Madeline Gardiner rose as her husband and other nieces entered the home. He had taken Kitty and Mary to the warehouses to pick out fabric for their wardrobes for the coming Season. The only reason Elizabeth had remained home was that Mr. Darcy had insisted on paying for all of her needs at the same modiste that served both Miss Darcy and Lady Matlock.

"Edward, how went the hunt?"

"Oh, Aunt, there was this most becoming emerald silk, but Uncle said you'd skin him alive if he allowed me to select such a color." Kitty pouted and looked at her uncle with dismay.

"Indeed she would!"

"But Mama is allowing Lydia to wear such shades. And she is not married!"

Madeline Gardiner pressed her mouth into a thin line of disapproval at the news of her sister-in-law's choice to indulge the youngest Bennet daughter, but quickly arranged her features to appease Kitty. Taking the young woman's arm to bring her further into the house, she gently stroked Kitty's forearm. "Yes, but Lydia will not be invited to so many balls and plays. You will be observing a full London season and just think how jealous Lydia will be of that!" Kitty began to nod her head but then stopped in her tracks. "I am to observe?"

Elizabeth rolled her eyes and blew out a breath. She knew this confrontation was coming, and as the eldest Bennet sister in residence, it shouldn't fall to her aunt to allay Kitty's immaturity. "Lady Matlock advised that we include you as we would Georgiana in society, a limited observance in anticipation of you enjoying a full coming out next Season."

Mary stepped forward to offer her own support of the plan, but the addition of Scripture didn't seem to help Kitty's disposition.

"So I'm to be the only sister not out? It's not fair!" Kitty's face clouded with anger and tears began to form. Mr. and Mrs. Gardiner shared a glance, and Mr. Gardiner wisely chose a stealthy retreat to his study. The women in the room surrounded the visibly upset Kitty and attempted to simultaneously ply her with positives in support of waiting to come out next Season. Still the young girl wailed and sobbed at the injustice of it all.

It appeared a bleak situation until Elizabeth looked up in frustration to see the butler tending to the doorbell, a sound she could barely hear over the cries of Kitty and compliments from her aunt and sister.

"Kitty! Look, that's Mr. Darcy here to take us all to Hyde Park. Go through the dining room to the kitchen and take the back stairs up to your room. Refresh your gown and hurry back so that we may all go enjoy the afternoon. Otherwise, you may find contentment by staying home."

Kitty immediately stopped crying. "Stay home? I do not wish to stay home. That's the point entirely!"

"Then go, quickly, before he sees you and asks why you're upset."

As Mr. Darcy and Miss Darcy were invited inside, the room seemed to have an odd sense of appearing too casual that made Darcy pause and take stock of the inhabitants. There was Elizabeth, glowing as always, though it appeared as if she had just been angry. Miss Mary wore a blank expression of indifference, and Mrs. Gardiner was radiantly enthusiastic in her welcome. He bowed as his sister curtsied and crossed the threshold.

"Is Miss Catherine not to join us?"

"Oh, she had a small accident with her dress and will be right down," Elizabeth said in a hollow and slightly higher-pitched voice than her normal tremor. "Georgiana, how lovely to see you! I hope you received the sheet music I sent?"

"Indeed, it arrived yesterday. Thank you for such a thoughtful gift!"

Elizabeth beamed at her soon-to-be younger sister. "When William and I were shopping for new books, I saw it in the music shop next door and knew you'd love the latest waltzes. I hear the dance is the highlight of every ball on the Continent."

Darcy cleared his throat and turned slightly red that Elizabeth had used his Christian name so casually. But perhaps it was safe enough here at the Gardiners', but he shuddered to think of what his cousins would say to him if she should slip at Matlock. Kitty rejoining the sitting room interrupted his worries, and he soon found the women all looking at him expectantly to follow them out to the carriage.

"Mrs. Gardiner, it is always a pleasure. I am saddened you could not join us this afternoon."

"I thank you, Mr. Darcy, but I believe a rest is most welcome to me this afternoon." She laughed as she allowed him to escort her to the hall where the younger ladies all congregated. "I trust you with my girls; please keep them safe."

"Always, madam. You have my word." Darcy bowed and helped the ladies into the carriage. As much as he wished to have joined them inside, he mounted Poseidon and rode alongside the carriage the number of blocks back towards the fashionable side of town.

❧ ❧ ❧ ❧ ❧ ❧ ❧ ❧ ❧

The picnic had barely been set when a bombastic voice called out to their group. "Darcy! You started without me, old man?" The Colonel walked with such pomp in full uniform up the path towards their little knell by the pond. While all of the ladies in attendance turned to see Colonel Fitzwilliam's approach, Elizabeth watched William's face as he pursed his lips for half a moment.

"Did you not wish for your cousin to come?" she whispered.

"No, I simply hoped his errands at the War Office would have lasted a little longer," he replied.

Elizabeth sat perplexed by Mr. Darcy's meaning until the introductions and greetings took her attention away. The Colonel happily sat himself between Kitty and Mary and quickly had all three of the younger girls giggling at some joke. "Colonel, I heard you just came from the War Office. I dare to hope you are not being called back to the front lines?"

The younger girls all shared a look of ghastly horror, but Richard nodded his head. "Sadly, it appears my Major General has high hopes for a title or two, and recently volunteered his units for another tour of duty. I won't abandon my men, so if they go, then I am afraid I must as well." Kitty let out a whimpered sigh at the Colonel's bravery and batted her eyelashes at the man. The Colonel looked at her for a brief moment, and disconcerted, he found his glass of wine poured by one of Darcy's servants and handed to him just before his pretty speech.

"Be truthful, Richard. You relish the excitement of going back. I posit you would agree to just about any scheme to get away from the balls and demands of your mother."

"Ho, ho, Darcy! Be not ruinous to the one trait I can claim above your wealth. My valor is above impunity."

"Surely, you are correct in that regard, but I also know your Major General gave you an opportunity to teach a future cavalry unit here. And you are vacillating between the two duties."

"I think there's great honor in a man who stays behind to train the men going to war. If they are not aptly prepared, their instructor is little more than a murderer, so the man who stays behind to train is of the highest honor, indeed." The entire group turned their heads to look at Mary after her sudden outburst, but Mary Bennet did not flinch, and instead she stared directly at the Colonel. The silence hung in the air for a few moments until the party began to busy themselves with eating. Kitty finally found a way to break the silence.

"Miss Darcy, would you like to take a stroll with me over the bridge? Would that be alright if we had a footman accompany us?"

"There's no need," Richard said as he stood and dusted the crumbs off his brilliant red coat, "I'll be happy to escort you ladies myself. Miss Mary?"

But Mary Bennet shook her head. "I should like to remain here, with my sister and Mr. Darcy."

"We hardly need a chaperone, Mary. Half of London is here today," Elizabeth tried to entice Mary to leave, but her sister wasn't budging. Giving up, Elizabeth turned to William. "Which two days was it again that your aunt suggested for the ceremony?"

Darcy loosened his cravat and leaned back on his hands. Snatching up a pretty red apple, he took a loud bite from it, garnering a soft giggle from Elizabeth. "She recommended either May 14th or May 21st so that we might travel to Scotland before

Sunday."

"And it takes three days to travel to your estate there?" Darcy nodded. "Well, I think you should tell her that if we can't manage it any earlier, then May 14th sounds like a perfectly lovely day to become Mrs. Darcy." She looked at Mr. Darcy and wiggled her nose like a bunny, their public gesture of affection ever since the dinner at her aunt and uncle's home. Darcy smiled widely at her, until suddenly his face soured. Walking back to their little picnic was the trio that had left to explore the path around the pond, but they had two extra in tow, Mr. Bingley and his sister Caroline.

"I fear we are about to be invaded," he whispered and Elizabeth's head whipped around to look behind her, then she quickly returned to look at her William.

Sighing, she supposed it was Miss Bingley's right to enjoy a public park on such a warm day, but she wondered what excuse Mr. Bingley would give for abandoning Jane in Hertfordshire? Plastering a smile in place, Elizabeth adjusted her seat to greet the advancing party.

"Miss Eliza! How splendid to find you in London and to think we nearly just missed you according to Miss Kitty. An Easter at Matlock, what a heavenly invitation for a family of such limited means." Miss Bingley allowed the Colonel to escort her to the blanket and she gracefully lowered herself to sit at Mary's feet. Elizabeth watched as Mary's legs involuntarily twitched every so slightly before her sister calmly tucked them up underneath her right side.

"Mr. Bingley, Miss Bingley. I hope the roads from Hertfordshire were kind? How are my mother and sisters?"

"Fine, fine, Miss Elizabeth, though Miss Lydia has been awfully ill of late. Poor Jane, I mean Miss Bennet, has been attending her and it was on her advice that we have taken the opportunity to visit London since she has not been able to entertain callers," Mr. Bingley said.

"Oh, dear, how ill is Lydia? We've heard no reports of this!" Mary said.

"She's probably fine, just pining away for Wickham. She's just pretending to be sick so she can keep getting sympathy."

"Kitty! We do not discuss that subject in public." Elizabeth hissed, as Caroline Bingley preened and smiled at the gossip. Elizabeth's stomach soured at the sight and turned to her finace. "Mr. Darcy, I'm afraid I am finding myself rather satisfied with Hyde Park. Perhaps another time we might visit with a gig?"

Darcy nodded and motioned for the servants to begin packing up.

"It was lovely to see you again, Mr. Bingley and Miss Bingley. I'd invite you to call, but I'm afraid we are to leave town just as you have arrived. A pity. I'm sure my aunt could use my help in preparing our dinner plans." Elizabeth plastered a smile in place as she farewelled the Bingleys, even as her blood began to boil that Charles would dare to abandon Jane because Lydia was ill.

"You're hosting a dinner? Are you having a large to-do?" Miss Bingley asked with a tone just asking for the guest list.

"No, just intimate friends and family, I'm afraid, though my brother, the Viscount, is attending." The

Colonel had endured enough of Caroline Bingley's barbs the entire walk back to the main group and felt little regret in putting her in her place, even if it meant he also slighted Bingley. Both Kitty and Mary looked at the Colonel with adoration, but it was Miss Mary he offered an arm to along with Miss Georgiana to help them back up the hill towards the Darcy carriage.

As Darcy and Elizabeth finished the farewells, Darcy made a point to offer his arm to Miss Kitty as well. Walking up the same hill as his cousin before him, Darcy wondered once more how he was going to warn the sisters to guard their tongues. Every scenario in his mind played with Elizabeth becoming so cross at him, he was at a loss for what he was to do. Ultimately, he decided once they returned to Gracechurch Street, he would have no choice but to ask Mr. Gardiner for his aid.

Chapter Eight

Throbbing pain in Elizabeth's temples made her happy to retire for a rest on the fourth afternoon at Matlock. Her feet ascended the thirty carpeted steps up the main hall as she still couldn't stop the details swirling in her mind for Easter dinner. Lady Matlock had helped her go through all of the escorts and privileges, but was Lady Sefton to be escorted in by Lord Marlborough or the Viscount of Eaton? She shook her head and remembered that Darcy's aunt was not going to let her fail.

The last room on the left in the visitor wing was hers, a completely separate hall from where Mr. Darcy was roomed on the family side of the mansion. With great effort, she pushed the heavy, medieval styled door and found Becky laying out her evening attire. Becky immediately curtsied, then seeing Elizabeth's color, she rushed forward to help her lady to her bed.

"A thousand thanks. Are there any powders left in my trunk?" Becky nodded and rushed to Elizabeth's private toiletry case to find the last packet of powders given to her by the apothecary in London. Without her habitual morning walk, the headaches Elizabeth sustained as a child were returning in full force. She was adamant that in the morning she would find a way to walk in the elegant gardens even if it meant she needed to tie the bed sheets and scale the balcony to avoid Lady Matlock and her endless teachings of running an estate the size of Matlock.

"Here you are, Miss Elizabeth. I'll send young Robin around to the town to purchase more. Mr. Darcy surely won't want you to be without your remedy."

"Please send a note to Mr. Darcy's valet that I intend to take a walk in the morning and would be so very pleased if his master would join me."

"Aye, ma'am." Becky curtsied and smiled. Knowing Miss Elizabeth since childhood had helped her tremendously in her transition from house maid to lady's maid. Though the rest of the above stairs staff at Matlock sniffed at her lack of credentials and formal training, she knew that Miss Elizabeth would never desire an unknown, snobby French maid, no how.

Elizabeth lay on the elegant cool sheets, wishing she could disrobe to her chemise, but if it was one thing she'd learned from her aunt before leaving, it was that house parties as large and elite as this one could quickly become dangerous grounds for maidens. She trusted Lady Matlock with her safety, but for the past two nights, she had not enjoyed the particular attentions of Lord Bergamote, a man of French ancestry staying with relations in Southern England, and she suspected that William had enjoyed those attentions even less so.

Rolling onto her side away from the door, she closed her eyes. Taking calming breaths, she willed the powders to begin working. After what felt like an eternity, she finally drifted off to sleep.

When Elizabeth woke hours later, the room was dark, and she cried out from fear of not knowing where she was. Her head still ached, but it was mostly a dull pain. Rubbing her eyes, she adjusted her vision to the darkened room and began to panic. She remembered where she was and threw the bed curtains to the side. How they had become closed, she didn't know, because she hadn't closed them. Stumbling around to light a candle, she called for Becky, but no answer came.

Finally lighting a candle, Elizabeth realized she was in her chemise and she hurriedly found her evening gown still laid out on the chair. Lady Matlock would be so furious with her if she had missed such an important dinner due to an inept servant. The disapproval from everyone she could imagine made her flustered, and she knocked the stack of books on her bureau while trying to reign in her unruly curls and wash her face off at the same time. She wasn't sure how she was going to secure the dress in the back and hoped Becky returned soon. The crash must have alerted others she was awake because her bedroom door opened a swift moment later and Mary rushed in.

"Lizzie, what on earth are you doing?"

"What does is appear that I am doing? I'm trying to hurry and dress for dinner! I'm so late!"

Mary clucked her tongue and gently pulled the hair brush from Elizabeth's hand. "It's eleven o'clock in the evening. I was just retiring when I heard the crash, and I worried you had fallen out of bed."

"I missed dinner?" Elizabeth cried, thoroughly panicked now. This was just like Netherfield all over again. She pressed her fingers to her head and cursed the plague of migraines that she inherited from Grandmother Bennet.

"Sssh, sssssh, it's all been resolved. When your maid told Mr. Darcy's valet you were ill, he asked me to see to you. You were writhing in pain, even as you slept, so Becky and I helped you undress as you did not wake. I made my report to Mr. Darcy and he decided that you were not to be disturbed."

"Oh, that's far worse!" Elizabeth began to pound her fists on her head, both to stop the buzzing and in complete frustration. Her first attempt and she had failed to be strong enough to play hostess.

Mary looked at Elizabeth with confusion. Her older sister was behaving most oddly, and she wasn't used to seeing the woman she looked up to so vulnerable. "Would you stop that caterwauling?" Shocked by the most impressive imitation of her father's favorite refrain, Elizabeth opened her teary eyes to look at Mary. "Have you completely lost your senses? Mr. Darcy was so caring and thoughtful to make sure you were attended and left to recover."

"Yet I have failed him! I keep trying to learn it all, but every day I am more and more confused. Just trying to remember the names of the maids who maintain the fireplaces over the maids who clean the linens and then there's the footmen for each room, and the menus, and the activities planned for each day. . ."

"Elizabeth Rose Bennet, you have gone over the moon. Get back into that bed this instant." Mary strong armed her sister to guide her to the bed and helped her out of the partially donned evening gown. "Lady Matlock is merely exposing you to what you will undoubtedly experience at Pemberley. You are not expected to run Matlock after only three days of instruction, nor will you be expected to run Pemberley. Lord have mercy, but did it not occur to you that Mr. Darcy's estate has run just fine without you lo these many years?"

Elizabeth blinked a few times and considered her sister's words. Of course Mr. Darcy's homes had run without a hitch before he met her. When had she thought to place all of this pressure on herself? Sighing, Mary became more tender and began to stroke the sweaty, matted hair from Elizabeth's forehead. "Are you hungry? I'll have Becky fetch a tray."

"Where is she? I called for her."

"She is downstairs with Molly and Sally learning from Lady Matlock's lady's maid. All of our maids Mr. Darcy hired are receiving instruction about the new expectations for our dress."

"Do not tax her then. I certainly don't want us both plagued with headaches. I shall simply eat a hearty breakfast." Mary nodded and found her way to the dressing room to remove her own dress. Elizabeth sat up in her bed on her elbows to see what Mary was doing. Mary shook her pinned hair out, and turned to look at Elizabeth as she placed it into a simple plait.

Shrugging, she looked down at her feet. "I know I'm not Jane. I just thought perhaps you'd prefer to not sleep alone tonight?"

Feeling the younger sister, even though she was not, Elizabeth grinned and nodded. Mary shared the giggle and hopped into bed to snuggle down in the cool sheets. As Elizabeth drifted off to sleep for the second time, her less pained mind began to wonder just when had Mary become so rational and how had she missed the transition?

❧ ❧ ❧ ❧ ❧ ❧ ❧ ❧ ❧

The next morning in London, Mrs. Gardiner wished her husband a great day at work and farewelled him after breakfast. Mr. Gardiner called the carriage as his business that morning would take him all the way to the docks as his second vessel was due to berth. Anchored in the channel, he had just paid the fees and wished to be present as full inventory of his wares from the boat to the warehouse were conducted. A key component to his family's success in trade was his fastidiousness in seeing to his own affairs, though he did include his head clerk, Albert, in learning the methods of his madness.

Pausing on the steps of his town home, Mr. Gardiner squinted at the bright sunlight piercing the dim fog that was so common. Tipping his hat to a passerby, he felt cheered that his wife had felt the movement of their fifth babe just that morning. With the expansion plans on his desk, he might be able to purchase a small estate for Madeline and the children in the next year or so. His jubilation added a bounce to his step as he took the four steps down to the street and addressed his driver before entering his carriage.

"Morning, Pierce," he said. Mr. Pierce, husband of the children's nanny, doffed his hat to his employer and made a low "Whoa," sound to keep the horses in line. They were already stamping their hooves and whinnying when he finally clicked his tongue to signal them to begin the drive.

The last thing Mr. Gardiner managed to do that morning was raise the shade before everything went terribly, terribly wrong. Just turning the second corner of his journey, his horses took off like a shot and he could hear yells and calls as the carriage took another turn before flipping onto its side and crashing. Mr. Gardiner tumbled inside of the carriage and thought he could somehow feel dirt on his face before he passed out.

A hundred miles away, Elizabeth Bennet and Mary Bennet were taking turns in Matlock's well manicured gardens when they came upon Colonel Fitzwilliam and Mr. Darcy. Elizabeth smiled and winked at her co-conspirator, and the girls happily separated to take the offered arms of the gentlemen.

"It would appear that those who rise the earliest enjoy the greatest peace," Mary remarked.

"Are you usually an early riser by rule, Miss Mary, or have you simply changed your habits due to the large nature of the party?"

"Neither. And it is impolite for you to inquire about my sleeping habits, sir," she said cooly, realizing the truth could not be the answer she gave.

The Colonel frowned at the sudden coyness of a lady he greatly admired, but knew for a man to understand the moods of a woman was a lost battle at its start. They remained silent for a spell after he apologized and walked a few paces behind the future Darcys.

"How are you this morning, my darling? I was so frightened that you were truly ill." Mr. Darcy jumped right to the subject Elizabeth had hoped most to avoid, and she sighed in response.

"I'm well. When I do not find a way to exercise, I suffer from debilitating headaches in the evening. It's a family trait, I'm afraid, and the real reason why I'm such a 'very accomplished walker.'"

"Hmm, perhaps in the future we shall find new forms of exercise to keep you well," Mr. Darcy mused in a near whisper, causing Elizabeth's breath to catch.

Her cheeks burning, she felt it wise to find a new line of discussion immediately. "Tell me about your parents. Did they have as long an engagement?"

"Longer, I'm afraid. My parents were an arranged marriage. The Matlock estate needed funds and my father had them. He was nearly fourteen years senior to my mother."

"Poor Lady Anne! Excuse me, I don't mean to say that your father was a poor match, but I don't know many young women who would relish marrying a man so much older."

Darcy shrugged his shoulders and whipped an errant weed with his walking stick. "No offense is taken. My parents were kind to one another, but they were not a love match. I am not ignorant that my father's many dalliances weighed heavily on my mother."

The brute honesty her future husband was sharing with her was a mild upset to Elizabeth, but then again, they had not enjoyed much time in private. Once they were married, they would have ample time for private conversation and his frankness would be a part of him to which she would become accustomed. As she looked over her shoulder, she could see that the Colonel and Mary were very far away and much further, they might be out of the bounds of propriety. "Mr. Darcy. . ."

"Fear not, we are safe. My cousin and I have an accord. And I suspect he might be attempting a small amount of courting himself."

Elizabeth giggled and covered her mouth. She found Mr. Darcy attempting to steer her towards a stone bench in the far corner, but her muscles were just feeling warmed up. Instead, she tugged his arm to beg another lap around the outside lane of the garden maze. "I thought Mary might be sweet on the Colonel, but lately, I'm not so sure."

"Well, I am confident my cousin can navigate the paths of his own love life. Tell me what led you to become so violently ill last night. I know you cannot be telling me all; you've missed your walk many a day during our engagement and I've never seen you so pale as yesterday afternoon."

Again, Elizabeth quickened her pace in agitation and didn't answer right away. "Elizabeth?" he asked, expectantly.

"Yes, I shall answer, I simply was commuting my feelings into words." She squeezed his arm with her own and noticed he smiled at her gesture. Bravely, she took a deep breath and released it. "I am afraid to say I am nervous about not measuring up to being the illustrious Mrs. Darcy. I shouldn't feel so, as my sister Mary pointed out last night that your homes have run just fine for many years without a mistress, but so much has changed for me, and more changes are on the horizon. Occasionally, my desire to be the very best person I can be turns into a dark and twisted voice of failure."

Immediately at her confession, Mr. Darcy stopped their forward progress and turned Elizabeth to face him. Frustrated that one of his hands still held his blasted walking stick, with his free hand he carefully stroked her cheek with the crook of his gloved finger. "You will always be the best wife for me. Never doubt."

Elizabeth closed her eyes and turned her chin up in hopes to feel the burn of Mr. Darcy's lips on her own, but the joking tone of the Colonel ruined the moment. The scowl on her face was most involuntary, but she schooled her expression before facing her future cousin.

"Ho, ho, good thing we arrived so quickly. Miss Mary, it appears we are the most perfect of chaperones there ever were." Richard smiled jovially to the young woman beside him, but Mary only gave him a half smile. Releasing her arm from the Colonel, she reclaimed her sister's arm in a clear signal the walk was over.

"And at least one of us will see to it that our chaperoning skills continue to keep young couples polite." Elizabeth couldn't help but giggle at her sister as she followed her lead and looked over her shoulder to wink at Mr. Darcy. The two gentlemen were standing in nearly the same spot as where they had met the young women, and they watched as their lithe forms crossed the grounds back towards the house.

"It would appear you are in trouble, Cousin." Mr. Darcy held his walking stick with both hands in front of him, content to wait a moment before following Elizabeth inside.

"Oh?"

"Yes, your lady is most vexed with you for leaving for war."

"Whenever did she say that?" The Colonel

frowned as he had listened most carefully to the few words he could get out of Miss Mary. Darcy merely tapped the side of his nose in a mimicry of Mr. Gardiner and finally began his own journey back to the house with hopes that he could organize a ride with some of the other gentlemen in attendance.

Chapter Nine

When the express reporting Mr. Gardiner's accident reached Fenley Cottage, it predictably sent Mrs. Bennet into near hysterics. "My brother is dead! How cruel to lose my husband and brother in one year! Must I endure the death of everyone I love?"

Jane ignored her mother's antics and paid the exhausted rider and directed him around to the back to find refreshment in the kitchen. As her mother continued to rant and rave, Jane managed to pry the missive from her flailing hands to read it for herself. Her eyes misted up as her aunt's shaky hand detailed there had been a ghastly carriage accident and that her uncle had several serious fractures in his right leg and was unconscious.

"Mother, Uncle Gardiner has not left us."

"But he will; oh, he will! He will never wake; I'm sure of it." Fanny Bennet continued to cry until she suddenly stopped and sat up from the newly ordered fainting couch in the sitting room. "I must away to my sister Phillips!"

"No, Mama. Lydia!" Jane shouted up the stairs to her youngest sister, who was spending more and more time in her bedroom. The youngest Bennet sister appeared atop the stairs and plodded down each step with a sour look on her face.

"What is it now? I was trying to rest."

Jane looked her sister up and down suspiciously, wondering where all of Lydia's abundant energy had disappeared to, then clucked her tongue. "We must ready the carriage. Uncle Edward has had an accident."

"La, we will just be in the way."

"Nonsense, our aunt could very much use our help. Prepare your trunk, and I shall pack mine and mother's."

"Ohh, I couldn't possibly go. My nerves cannot bear to see him die! You must go Jane and represent the family. Do as you must. And be sure to let Mr. Bingley know you have arrived. It's such a pity he had to rush off to London for business again."

Lydia flounced into the sitting room and lounged on the overstuffed arm chair with her legs dangling over the side. "I shan't go either; someone must stay home with poor Mama."

White-hot anger spread through Jane's body as her hand involuntarily crumpled her aunt's message. Seething with rage, all Jane Bennet could do was breath in and out before she curtsied and took the stairs to her own room. Where she could not trust her tongue, she resolved to keep it out of use. As she packed her gowns and personal effects, she chastised herself for not standing up to her mother and younger sister. In her mind all of the rejoinders and harsh criticisms those two women needed to hear played over and over, and Jane hated herself for never wishing to rock the boat. Mr. Bingley hadn't left for London on business. She had sent him away when he hinted at his boredom to avoid further embarrassing displays. And his sister! The way Caroline Bingley appeared to inspect every inch of the cottage and her younger sister's illnesses, Jane didn't know what Caroline's game was, but she agreed with Elizabeth that she was not a woman to be trusted.

The fury of her anger had made short work of her labor and within the hour her trunk was packed and the carriage ready. Her mother and sister did not even deign to step outside and wish her farewell, and as the carriage rolled away towards London, Jane Bennet suspected today was the first day of finding her own future.

🦋 🦋 🦋 🦋 🦋 🦋 🦋 🦋 🦋

For two days, Elizabeth had many assurances from Lady Matlock to not distress over falling ill. Still, she couldn't shake the feeling she was in the woman's debt, so she offered to help oversee the dinners and activities. Without a pounding headache plaguing her, Elizabeth made short work of the menu and memorizing the table seating assignments. All had gone on without a hitch until the gentlemen joined the ladies the night before half of the party planned to break off and visit Pemberley.

Excitement bubbled in Elizabeth's chest as she tried to stay occupied on the last night of her stay at Matlock. Seated on a settee with Georgiana and Kitty, Elizabeth had been enjoying Kitty telling her all about the latest chapter in her novel. Georgiana frequently interrupted, reminding Kitty of the parts she was leaving out and Elizabeth found the antics of the two young ladies highly amusing.

"And then, the dastardly cousin, who inherited the estate, tries to compromise poor Sarah, but the steward she is in love with rushes into the room and saves the day. But, of course, now he is dismissed from his duties, and Sarah is crying at how much she will miss her sisters as she packs a trunk. . ." Kitty trailed off as a shadow fell over their small group from behind Elizabeth's back. Elizabeth turned around expecting Mr. Darcy, but instead her smile faded away as once more it was Lord Bergamote seeking her out.

He bowed very low and offered his hand. "Miss Elizabeth, it would be my greatest pleasure to escort you to Lady Matlock. She has requested your presence."

Twisting her lips in disapproval, Elizabeth had little choice but to accept the Frenchman's hand and cringe as he took the longest way possible around the room to the sofa where Lady Matlock and Lady Sefton were seated.

"Thank you, Antoine." Lady Sefton waived her hand, and Lord Bergamote bowed lowly to the grand dame. With the piercing stare of an owl, the patroness of Almack's looked Elizabeth up and down, seemingly inventorying every thread of the burgundy gown Elizabeth had chosen for the evening's repast. "Not a classic beauty, no, but I do see some of the spark you mentioned, Maggie."

Instead of appearing offended, Elizabeth smiled and inspected Lady Sefton right back. "How is your evening, Lady Sefton? I am so pleased to make your acquaintance on this first visit to Matlock."

"Tell me, Miss Elizabeth, how many sisters do you have in total? I've heard six mentioned."

Elizabeth shook her head. "I'm afraid not, madam, I am in possession of only four sisters at the moment, but I look forward to claiming a fifth very soon."

"And all of you are out in society? With you engaged before the eldest? And the youngest too I hear? How very strange. Your mother and father must not keep careful control of their household."

Elizabeth looked to Lady Matlock, who merely took the moment to drink her tea, but Elizabeth noticed the slight twitch in her ladyship's mouth. "Indeed, your Ladyship, though my poor father passed away last autumn, my sisters and I have enjoyed very little time to mourn or grieve before my cousin inherited our estate and cast us out. My eldest and youngest sisters are both in courtships with gentlemen, but I was fortunate enough to receive Mr. Darcy's love and admiration. Jane would never wish to delay my happiness for the privilege of marrying first."

"Hmph. In my day, there was no talk of love with marriage. You married the match selected by your elders and remained in your own sphere."

Elizabeth cleared her throat and cocked her head to one side. "Surely, my ladyship, you are not suggesting I have quit my own sphere by marrying Mr. Darcy? He is a gentleman and I am a gentleman's daughter. In that so far we are equal. That he also is a man I most highly esteem and admire are additional inducements."

"And I'm sure the prize of Pemberley never crossed your mind in considerations?"

Lady Matlock interjected before Elizabeth could completely lose her temper. "Actually, Agatha, Miss

Bennet has not yet seen Pemberley, though she is to visit on the morrow. Perhaps you might remind Georgiana and Miss Catherine they ought to retire."

Slowly rising and quitting the two grand ladyships in the room, she hoped she had made Lady Matlock proud. Elizabeth glanced around the room and still saw no sign of the Fitzwilliam brothers, Mr. Darcy, or the Earl. Just as she reached her sisters, the loud bombastic voice could be heard from the Earl as the Colonel opened the doors to enter the room.

"You will march back here this instant. I have not finished my say!" Colonel Fitzwilliam gallantly bowed to the room at large and continued his paces towards Miss Mary. He stopped mid-room when his father continued his tirade. "Richard Bartholomew, I can still turn you over my knee!"

Winking at Mary, who frowned at him, Richard turned around to face his father, who was beet red in the face. "I should like to see you try to best one of His Majesty's Finest."

"Reginald! Richard! What is all of this about?" Lady Matlock rose to stand between her son and husband, as the rest of the room began to settle in for the show. Quickly Elizabeth whispered to Georgiana and Kitty that they needed to retire, and both girls started to pout until Elizabeth's eyes bulged to emphasize her request was not a suggestion. The two young girls slipped out of the room just as the male voices continued to rise in the room.

Sitting next to Mary, Elizabeth reached over to grip her younger sister's hand as she was wringing both of them in her lap. "What is the matter?"

"He did not tell his parents he was volunteering to go back to the front."

"Oh dear."

The two Bennet sisters watched as the Fitzwilliam family had their drama out in front of all. The Viscount, for his part, supported his younger brother, but the Earl took it as a slap in the face that his own son would rebuff his father's care and support if he would just give up his commission.

"You've played soldier and done admirably in the ranks. Now it's time to take your place in society, be a Fitzwilliam, and live up to your responsibilities." The Earl paced the elegantly tatted carpet in front of the hearth, appearing as a lion caged.

"You've mixed your metaphors, father. I did not join the Navy."

"Confound it, boy, this is serious."

"Indeed, I take my life and responsibilities very seriously. If you and Mother see fit to cut me off, then I respect your decision. But I, who have seen the true horrors of war and what that tyrant has imparted on our European brethren, will not stand idly by to see the ravages reach my homeland. No, sir." The Colonel stood as erect as a call to attention and did not waiver as his father's face slackened in shock, then his lips moved wordlessly as a fresh wave of anger now colored his cheeks a hideous shade of purple.

Elizabeth squirmed in her seat and looked to find Mr. Darcy, but his eyes were not on her. She noticed he too was looking at Richard and his facial expression was not one of kindness.

"Of course we will not cut you off, dear." Lady Matlock moved to slide her arm into her son's elbow. "But let's save all of this unpleasantness for tomorrow when we can discuss it as a family without burdening our guests. Reginald? I find that I am dreadfully exhausted from today's endeavors. Shall we retire?" Lady Matlock briefly rubbed her son's arm, then detached herself from him to glide over to her husband and slide her arm into his. The poor Earl was still at a loss for words as his wife guided him towards the stairs.

Finally, Elizabeth captured Mr. Darcy's attention, and he joined her side. "Do you care to retire as well, or perhaps stay up a little longer?"

Honestly, Elizabeth was exhausted, and she did not care for the way Lord Bergamote still eyed her from his far corner of the room. With her largest ally in the room gone, she had no desire to cross swords with Lady Sefton again.

"I believe I should like to get some extra rest for our journey tomorrow. I know it's but a half day's ride, but I would hate for the staff of Pemberley to see me looking less than my best." Elizabeth smiled at Darcy to show him she was being light-hearted and not falling back into the melancholy of worrying about expectations.

"I bow to your wise decision, madam. Would you permit me to escort you?"

Her hand shaking, Elizabeth accepted Mr. Darcy's arm, and they too quitted the room. She worried that it was most unbecoming to have him escort her out, and the beady eyes of Lady Sefton took great notice. All of these thoughts distracted her until they arrived at her bedroom door far too quickly than she recalled the walk to be.

"William. . ., " she said timidly.

"Elizabeth," he replied, huskily.

Without warning, he swept her into his arms

and embraced her with all of his might. Feeling a tad pinched, her squeak reminded him to lessen his grip, and he stepped away in embarrassment.

"No, please, I'm sorry." She reached out, and her hand slid down his coat sleeve until she could finally grip his hand. The flesh on flesh connection made them both pause, and he gently squeezed her hand. She sighed, and Mr. Darcy bowed deeply over her hand and kissed it.

"Good night, my darling. Tomorrow I shall show you my world and all I can offer a beauty such as yourself."

As he stepped away from her, she held his gaze. Feeling brazen, she lifted her fingers to her lips and kissed them before opening her hand in his direction. Not brave enough to see his response, Elizabeth hurriedly opened her door and rushed inside. Her heart aflutter, it wasn't until she was trying to find sleep that she began to worry about Mary.

❦ ❦ ❦ ❦ ❦ ❦ ❦ ❦ ❦

For hours it seemed the staff and occupants of Matlock House were in a flurry. Lady Sefton's group was to leave first, though the woman had changed her date of departure at the last moment, forcing the Darcy group to await her pleasure. It was nigh upon noon before her carriages were packed and gone from the lane and Darcy's own carriages could be packed and readied.

"At this rate, we'll be lucky to reach Pemeberley before dark." Mr. Darcy growled as he looked at the high position of the sun. Elizabeth linked her arm into his and smiled.

"It shall be fine, William. We have a few days at Pemberley before we must be back in London for the engagement schedule your aunt has put together."

"Yes, remind me to thank her ever so much for back to back teas and balls in the first days of our return."

His fiancee erupted into giggles and her mirth at his sourness began to melt the aggravation of leaving later than he had planned. The two of them began to lose themselves in each other on the grand steps of the Matlock Estate as a cloud of dust heralded the arrival of a single rider entering the lane. With all of the Bennet sisters and Miss Darcy, plus Lord and Lady Matlock outside, the head footman rushed forward to greet the express rider and receive his missive before pointing him towards the stables. Smoothing his livery, the footman handed the note with his white gloves to Lady Matlock. She opened it and swiftly read the contents.

"No!" she gasped, handing the letter to her husband. He also read the note and took a deep breath. Approaching his nephew and his intended, the Earl coughed slightly to break the gazes of Elizabeth and William.

"It appears there has been an accident and your uncle was seriously injured. I'm truly sorry."

The Earl handed the note to Elizabeth and bowed. Her hands shaking, Elizabeth accepted the note and read to the point of where her aunt described her uncle's accident before she cried out and dropped the letter. Mary stepped forward as Elizabeth turned to Darcy's arms for support, but the Colonel reached the letter first.

"Please, allow me." The Colonel read the note

and offered his arm to Mary. "Your Uncle Gardiner lives, but his carriage crashed some four days ago in London. The Bennets are asked to gather back in Cheapside"

"How could two tragedies strike our family so suddenly?" Kitty wailed. Georgiana embraced her friend and confidante.

"Sssh, sssh, the counsel of the Lord standeth for ever, the thoughts of his heart to all generations," Georgiana said in a soft tone, trying to provide comfort.

For a few minutes the party seemed frozen, stunned at the news and reflecting on the scripture quoted by the youngest of their family. Finally the Colonel broke the spell.

"Right. Givens, Hampton, take the Bennet luggage and put it all on this carriage. Move all of the Darcy luggage to that carriage."

"Richard! Those are my carriages!"

"Holmes!" The butler of Matlock House appeared from just inside the house. Colonel Fitzwilliam continued his barking orders. "Tell Mr. Pratt to pack my belongings, we leave in fifteen minutes."

"Richard! A moment of discussion if you please." Darcy shouted, finally getting his cousin's attention.

"Leave it, Darce. You must go to Pemberley, you told me as much last evening. It's been months. I shall escort the Miss Bennets to London, and you and Georgiana can meet us in a fortnight."

"But—"

"Now, let's show these ladies inside and perhaps give them a moment or two of refreshment?" The Colonel ignored his younger but wealthier cousin and offered his arm to Miss Catherine so that she could be escorted in as he still held Miss Mary's arm. The Earl nodded to his son in respect and followed his lead. Stuck without a better idea, Darcy had no choice but to escort Elizabeth and Georgiana inside.

As they climbed the stairs, he whispered to Elizabeth. "I am sorry, but he is right. I've been away for half a year, and there are responsibilities I cannot put off any longer."

"It's perfectly fine, William. I will miss you, but I know you will hurry to London as soon as you are able."

Releasing Georgiana's arm so that she could precede them inside, Darcy took a moment to lock eyes with Elizabeth, who was still tearing up.

"You have my word."

Chapter Ten

Smug satisfaction dissolved to tediousness as George Wickham shuffled up the worn steps to Sally Younge's boarding house in the wee hours of the morning. Finished with his duties for the day, he was dog tired, wanting nothing more than a hot meal and his bed. Unfortunately, there was Mrs. Younge, tapping her foot, waiting for him in the foyer.

"You've lied to me." Her eyes slanted, she crossed her arms in front of her chest. "Those Bennet girls have been back in town for over a week! Where's the one you fancied? Nab her and be done with it, so Mr. Darcy hastens to pay you off."

Wickham yawned. "She did not leave her mother. Only the older four are in town." He smiled slightly as he thought to himself that if he were Lydia, he would have avoided the work as well. The older Bennet girls all left at sunup to hurry to their Uncle's warehouse and rarely returned until nearly sunset. He couldn't see Lydia Bennet being much help in such circumstances unless they desired an orchestra of complaints each day.

"You said this would work. You said if the uncle was injured they would all rush to London."

Wickham shrugged and tried to walk past her, but Sally Younge slammed her hand to the wood door frame and blocked his way. "These dalliances of yours, they're pennies compared to the pay off we both deserve. Find a way to fix this, or find another place to stay." She glared at him menacingly, and the tall, dumb footman she kept near her side seemingly appeared out of nowhere.

With a flash of charm, George smiled and ducked under her arm. "Careful now, there will be none of that. Threats aside, you need me, Sally girl, or you have nothing on old Darcy." Whistling a bar tune, Wickham also sleazed by the footman back towards the kitchens. He knew it wouldn't be much longer that he could keep her happy, but as long as she needed him, he would be safe. Once she tired of this scheme, he had better be long on his way. Sally Younge did not keep many witnesses to her dealings, and he knew too much with too little of her heart attached to him.

꿩 꿩 꿩 꿩 꿩 꿩 꿩 꿩 꿩

The bell above the door rang in the large warehouse on Cordwainer Street. Elizabeth Bennet wiped her sweaty brow, inadvertently swiping a black line of dust across her forehead. With another heave, she moved the crate in front of her to a stack next to her and used a crowbar to pry the lip of the top lid. The tall visitor made his way to her and in the dust-fairy filled grayish sunlight, she knew right away that profile was none other than her intended.

"William!" she shouted and grinned as she sashayed around the maze of crates, but stopped just before him as she self-consciously realized she was quite filthy.

"This is where I find you? Aunt Maggie has been beside herself that she has had to make regrets for you at numerous teas and parties you promised to attend."

Elizabeth lifted the corner of her apron to wipe her hands. "I've sent notes to Lady Matlock to send my regrets in advance! I couldn't possibly sit in a parlor, sipping tea, while my Uncle recovers and there is so much work to be done."

"Work! You are a gentlewoman! Does not your Uncle hire enough staff to manage his affairs?" Darcy scoffed at the room around him as he finally looked at the tasks where her other sisters were employed. Mrs. Gardiner, very round in her midsection, walked with a board and made notations over each crate the ladies opened, various shop boys ran around opening crates for the ladies and moving them. Only his fiance was taking it upon herself to work alone. He shook his head. "Forgive me, madam, for taking up so much of your time. My presence here is unwanted and unnecessary." He bowed and began to walk away.

"William!" Elizabeth cried out, feeling very frustrated that she had protected her family and, in the process, offended her fiance. She started to walk after him, but his longer gait was too long when he wished it so. By the time she caught up, he was already out the door and stepping back into his carriage. She watched the equipage roll away, slowly feeling her embarrassment turn to anger. If he couldn't see the good in what she was doing, then perhaps it was best he leave and play the dandy. She had no time for such frivolous men in her life.

The Darcy carriage rolled to a halt in Mayfair and no sooner had Fitzwilliam entered his domicile than the tinkling piano music stopped and his younger sister Georgiana rushed to the foyer. "William, you are back so soon! Could you not find Elizabeth?"

"Oh, I found her! First, I attended the tea Aunt advised me was set for today in her letter. I sat for twenty minutes listening to those old harpies ruminate about the size of my purse and person and then toss slyly derogatory remarks about Elizabeth's absence. I hastened to the Gardiner home, but she was not there, either. Finally, a stable hand, of all people, tipped me off that all of the Miss Bennets were working in the warehouse from dawn to dusk!" Darcy walked past his sister to his study to pour himself a drink. She followed him.

"But, I don't understand. You are here. And she is there?"

Darcy knocked back the brandy and wiped his mouth, then straightened his cravat. "Oh, I expressed my displeasure. I am assured she will think twice before resuming these tradesmen duties." Georgiana slanted her eyes at her brother and huffed out.

"Marlborough!" she shouted, "tell them to bring the carriage back around!"

"Georgiana!" Darcy exclaimed, in shock that his sister would dare to raise her voice in the household. "Where on earth are you off to?" He walked out of the study to see her donning her bonnet and sliding on her gloves.

"Where you ought to be, Brother."

"But... I said... you couldn't possibly be thinking ... " Darcy squeezed his eyes shut and pinched them with his right fingers. How? How was he cursed with two headstrong women in his life? He felt Georgiana approaching him and opened his eyes.

With her beautiful brown eyes, she pouted with the practice of a young girl accustomed to manipulating the men around her. Her voice, however, dripped with venom. "She needed you. You abandoned her." She shook her head and walked out the door that the butler now held open.

Exasperated, Darcy picked up his cane and hat from the front table and followed his sister. The entire carriage ride, she refused to speak to him, and Darcy's mind began to reel at the set down he was about to experience. The more and more he played the facts of the situation in his mind, the more his behavior abhorred him. He had indeed allowed the matrons of society to cloud his judgment so poorly that, in the process, he had hurt the one person he cared for the most.

As the Darcy carriage returned to Cordwainer Street, Georgiana made sure to be handed out of the carriage first, nearly knocking her brother back into his seat. He groaned at the physical message she was sending to him and prepared himself for the worst.

Once inside, the Bennet girls hastened to welcome Georgiana, and as she explained why she had come, Mary wasted no time in finding her closest friend an apron to protect her gown. Darcy stood and watched the miraculous efficiency of the women -- the hustle and bustle of the warehouse did not cease for one instant, and any kind command they gave, the shop boys expeditiously carried out. It truly was a marvel, but his more balanced observations were interrupted.

"Lizzie is in the office. I believe you two could use some privacy," Mrs. Gardiner said, then scurried right past him to help Georgiana with what looked like a crate of cosmetics. He snatched his hat off of his head to hold it in front of him and hesitantly took a few steps towards the office. Inside, Elizabeth was furiously writing. Papers of sums and figures laid scattered on the desk.

"Elizabeth?" She ignored him, so he tried again, approaching the desk this time. "My darling, please forgive me." She continued to scratch her thoughts, then threw the pen down. Leaning back in the chair, much reminiscent of her uncle, the fierce look on her face took him aback.

"What can I help you with, Mr. Darcy? As you can see, we are quite busy this afternoon."

At a loss for more to say, he took the seat in front of the desk. "I . . ." He inhaled a deep breath. "I was wrong to chastise you. You, who are so kind and sweet, of course. there was no choice but for you to help the family that took you in, your poor relations in trade."

She arched her eyebrow. "My poor relations in - - "

"What I mean is your relations in trade. They certainly are not poor, but they are not as high in society, of course, but then again . . . ." he stammered and struggled to clarify his thoughts.

"Mr. Darcy, I am confused. Yes, you were wrong, but if you still look down on my Aunt and Uncle Gardiner, then, sir, I am at a loss for what our future could possibly be. These people you so naturally dismiss are paragons of virtue. Good day, sir." She resumed her scribbling, leaving Mr. Darcy dumbstruck in his seat.

For a few moments, neither said anything until Darcy shook his head. How had the world become so topsy-turvy to him? This was unacceptable. And he would not be the one dismissed! He was a gentleman. As he now saw it, there were gentlewomen who needed his help. He stood and noticed Elizabeth flicked her eyes up for a briefest moment, then resumed her purposeful disregard of his person. He removed his coat, tugged off his cravat and placed them on his chair. Again he noticed she glanced his way while trying to hide her interest. No matter, he thought and actually began to smile as he rolled up his shirtsleeves.

"Words are rarely the best act of contrition. Direct me, madam, and I shall not fail you a second time."

Amused, Elizabeth's mouth twisted to hide her smile. She tilted her head and motioned towards the door. "Go earn your forgiveness, sir, and you shall have it."

As her fiance bowed, Elizabeth held her breath and prayed that the true man she was marrying was the one marching out to assist and not the one who blasted her family with the prejudices of society. Resuming her attention to her sums, she also hoped her aunt would assign him to the spice crates. A little dose of pepper oils would be a suitable punishment. Imaging his nose red and eyes watering, she laughed and returned to adding up the receivables against the master manifest. Her neck ached and her fingers burned, but she was determined that soon they would finish this nasty business of inventory.

᪥ᩔ ᪥ᩔ ᪥ᩔ ᪥ᩔ ᪥ᩔ ᪥ᩔ ᪥ᩔ ᪥ᩔ ᪥ᩔ

For three days, Georgiana and Darcy assisted in the warehouse, and Darcy had even gone so far as to review the financial documentation with Mr. Gardiner's head clerk and visit with the sick man himself. Mr. Bingley had called at the Gardiner home, but as he was told the ladies were not available for callers, he had simply shuffled away. It was on the second evening after the inventory was complete that he finally ran into Darcy at their mutual club, though Darcy looked worse for the wear.

"Aye, Darcy, I say, has Harding bested you in fencing again?" Bingley pounced on the open armchair next to his friend.

Darcy shook his head and sipped his drink. With a low voice, he explained why he was so sore and tired from the warehouse work. The look of shock mixed with terror on Bingley's face froze the conversation for a spell. After a loud crack from the fireplace, Darcy politely asked why Bingley never showed up to help.

"Ah," Bingley rubbed the back of his neck with his hand, "I called a number of times, but each visit the butler told me the ladies were unavailable for callers. I assumed Mr. Gardiner's injuries were still of a serious nature."

Darcy looked flabbergasted at his friend. "Charles, unavailable means the servant is telling you there is something wrong. If he had said they were not accepting calls, that would mean you've personally been barred access."

"Oh." Bingley looked around the room in an attempt to lessen his embarrassment. "How in blazes was I supposed to know?" Looking into his own glass, Bingley shook off his faux pas and chuckled. "At least it saved me from the stink of trade again, eh?"

Darcy shrugged. He would never admit his own first error, and he was surprised at how repulsed he felt from Bingley's own careless prejudices, though his fortune actually came from trade. Bingley's father had been in the wool trade, so it was more than just prejudice but actual hypocrisy. "Tomorrow I am to escort Miss Elizabeth to Hyde Park on a picnic. Perhaps you'd care to join me to call on Miss Bennet?"

Again Bingley's face turned a deep shade of red. "Tomorrow? No, I don't believe, that is . . . Caroline has arranged a luncheon that I really mustn't miss."

"She didn't perchance invite some ladies to this luncheon, did she? Perhaps Miss Graham and Lady Towsend?"

"How did you...? I'll be dashed you don't have a secret network of spies."

"Stand down, Bingley, I have no such thing. Did it not occur to you that your sister would also invite me? I asked Elizabeth if she and Jane were invited, and finding they were not, I properly filed the invitation in my fireplace."

"Now, Darcy, my sister means well . . ."

"Don't be deuced, Charles." Darcy stood and stretched his aching muscles, then motioned to the man in the room for his personal effects. "You need to stop being such a whelp and make a decision in regards to Miss Bennet. As my future sister-in-law, I take any man who would dally with her affections very seriously. In two weeks there is to be a ball on the eve of my nuptials to Miss Elizabeth. It is the last invitation I will force my aunt to make to both Bingleys, if you catch my drift, unless there is a connection that cannot be ignored."

Darcy bowed and took his leave when his effects arrived and hoped that Elizabeth would be happy with his interference. She was right that this courtship of theirs had tarried on far too long, and it needed to be broken or cemented to help prevent talk of Lydia.

Chapter Eleven

With two weeks left until her wedding, Elizabeth Bennet was once again packing her trunks. This time, she and Mary were to reside with Lady Matlock until the wedding ceremony in order to lessen the strain on the Gardiner home. Jane elected to remain behind to provide extra help, though Elizabeth secretly suspected that society was steadily becoming her elder sister's least favorite part of living in London. Gone were the plethora of compliments and attentions she enjoyed in Meryton. At the few teas the girls had attended, the main focus was always on Elizabeth, a status the second oldest Bennet sister was not keen to continue but had little choice in the matter.

Accepting another gown from her aunt, Elizabeth graciously thanked her. "It seems I cannot stay put in one household for more than a month!" The two women shared a giggle. Mrs. Gardiner took a seat on the bed, careful not to sit on any of the garments already laid out.

"I'm afraid it's about to become much worse for you, my dear. The post of Mrs. Darcy requires extensive travel and packing."

Elizabeth made a face and lowered the burgundy dress she was in the process of folding. "I do hope there will be other inducements." For a moment, the two women remained completely serious, but soon broke into laughter. Mrs. Gardiner patted her niece's hand, happy that her private talks with her niece had made Elizabeth look forward to the wedding bed, not fear it.

"My dear, I do believe at this time in just a few weeks you will be quite the content wife. Now, if you'll excuse me, I must return back downstairs. Jane is entertaining the Bingleys."

"Pray, I fear my packing will take me much longer that I originally expected."

Mrs. Gardiner clucked her tongue and shook her head. "Oh be hidden with you. Poor Jane does not need you sparring with Miss Bingley this afternoon."

Shrugging, Elizabeth returned to her packing, tucking her father's copy of Hamlet into its usual place. The tome had become quite the travel companion and its addition to her trunk made her smile wistfully, remembering that night only a few months ago when she had imagined packing for the life of a spinster. Here she was packing for her life as a wife, and she found the latter much more to her liking, even if she did dislike packing in general.

Downstairs, Jane struggled with the Bingleys' visit.

"And Lord Bergamot is quite the gentleman! Being from France, he has such a number and variety of bon mots that we were all in stitches at Lady Carrigan's, were we not, Charles?" Caroline Bingley continued to bring up subjects Jane could not possibly remark on.

"He was not so witty," Charles sniffed, noticing Jane was scarcely paying attention. The more he considered making good on Darcy's warning, the less confident he was that he could give Jane a happy life. "But let's have no more talk of balls! Have you considered my invitation to the theater, Miss Bennet?"

Before Jane could answer, the front door to the Gardiner house opened and a very loud and shrill Lydia Bennet arrived in the front foyer.

"La, where is everyone? Let me go. It's me, Lydia! I am the niece engaged to the wonderful Mr. Wickham. Isn't he here as well?"

Jane blanched as Caroline reached for her teacup in a knowing manner. "Pardon me, Miss Bingley, Mr. Bingley." Jane rose from her seat as Mr. Bingley stood and bowed. Both Mrs. Gardiner and Jane reached Lydia at the same time, and the drastic plumpness of her figure made both women pause and look at one another in horror.

"We had no idea you were to travel. Why did you send no note?" Mrs. Gardiner's voice was strained as she mentally worked out where to place Lydia, then remembered that Mary and Elizabeth were to leave that very afternoon.

"And ruin the surprise? Where is he? Surely he's been found by now!"

"Lydia, Mr. Wickham is not here," Jane explained quietly.

Suddenly, a look of panic crossed Lydia's face, and she began to shout. "What do you mean he is not here? It's been months, Mr. Darcy promised he would find him! He must be found!"

Mrs. Gardiner and Jane shared another glance,

and Mrs. Gardiner wrapped her arm around Lydia, attempting to steer her towards the back of the house, but Lydia refused to move and fought her guidance. Jane rushed back to the sitting room.

"Mr. Bingley and Miss Bingley, it appears my sister has traveled from Hertfordshire to surprise us and see to her Uncle, but she is greatly fatigued. You'll forgive me for asking your pardon. I promise to call upon you in the very near future?"

Caroline Bingley sniffed, but placed her teacup down and rose with her brother. "Of course, Jane dear, we could not possibly impose on you at a time like this."

Jane gave both a relieved smile, but as she walked them to the door, Mrs. Gardiner and Lydia were still in the foyer. As Caroline Bingley looked Lydia up and down, saying nothing, the bottom of Jane's stomach dropped. She wasn't positive, but any woman would take one look at Lydia Bennet and come to only one conclusion. The youngest Bennet daughter was breeding.

Not long after the Lydia ruckus and the Bingley departure, the Matlock carriage arrived. With Mrs. Gardiner busy in the kitchen plying a crying Lydia with tea and comfort, Jane Bennet began to weep in the armchair just inside of the drawing room. When the carriage was announced and her other sisters beginning to descend the stairs, Jane wiped her eyes as quickly as she could and set her shoulders back. She was the eldest Bennet sister, and already too much had fallen onto Elizabeth's shoulders to fix. With a serene smile, she greeted her sisters at the bottom of the stairs.

"Have a lovely time and make sure to tell Lady

Matlock how much I appreciate her invitation." Jane hugged Elizabeth farewell.

With a quizzical expression, Elizabeth looked around in the hallway, but could only hear soft voices from the kitchen. "Is Aunt crying?" Elizabeth began to take a few steps towards the back of the town home, but Jane blocked her way.

"Sssh, Aunt is embarrassed that her sentiments have run away again, but she said she will see you both soon. It would not be prudent to make the Matlocks wait."

Elizabeth eyed her sister suspiciously, but shook her head. The Jane she knew and loved was not the same Jane that left their mother's house to come to London, but there was no doubt any intrigues between Jane and their aunt were of a good nature. In fact, Elizabeth wondered if the two of them did not have some surprise planned for her as that was certainly what she would be doing if their positions were reversed. Turning around and linking arms with Mary, Elizabeth Bennet took her final steps across the Gardiner threshold as a resident.

Once the carriage had safely rolled away, Jane turned from the front window and hastened to the kitchen. Lydia looked forlornly at the table, still heaving sporadically with dry sobs. Covering her mouth in horror, she looked at her aunt for confirmation, and her aunt slowly nodded.

"Mr. Wickham must be found straight away, I'm afraid," was all her aunt explained with a heavy tone.

Gingerly, Jane approached Lydia to sit next to her, and the younger girl lifted her head to stare at her oldest sister with red-rimmed eyes. "I'm to be married. He said, he said—" she gulped for air, "he said we were to be married." Finished, she wailed a new howl of anguish.

Overwhelmed with grief for her sister, and all of their futures, Jane embraced Lydia and pulled her to her chest. "Shhh, shhh, all will be well. You were very brave to travel here all alone. Very brave. Together we will find a way to protect you and the baby. I promise."

Mrs. Gardiner excused herself and shuddered as she bristled down the hallway. She wished she could share Jane's optimism, but without a trace of Mr. Wickham, and the family more or less deciding there was no future for Lydia married to that lout, she was unsure how they might find protection for anyone. With a deep breath, she took the stairs one at a time to avoid for as long as possible the moment when she must break her husband's heart.

※ ※ ※ ※ ※ ※ ※ ※ ※

Arriving at the Matlock house, Mary and Elizabeth were handed down by two of the most dashing Fitzwilliam men. The Colonel was on hand to escort Miss Mary as his cousin, Mr. Darcy was there to enjoy the attentions of his intended.

"The ride was not too taxing, I hope?"

Elizabeth playfully swatted Mr. Darcy's arm and laughed. "Hardly, sir. Now the constant packing and unpacking of trunks on the other hand, that is quite taxing indeed." Darcy gave her a look of pure chagrin.

"I could have sent Becky to your aunt's home. I was merely acquiescing to your request that she not permanently join your service until we are wed."

Elizabeth sighed. "And I still believe that was

for the best. This Mrs. Darcy business is quite overwhelming at present, and I am following the advice of my betters."

"Oh?" The couple finally began to walk towards the townhome, following the Colonel and Mary.

"Yes. I will only take on those duties and delights as I am comfortable with, no more, no less."

"Hmm, very wise." Darcy leaned close to Elizabeth's ear just as they reached the door. "I promise to make you quite comfortable, Mrs. Darcy." With a nonchalant expression, Darcy handed a red faced Elizabeth into the foyer, and if she gave a little shiver before her curtsy to Lady Matlock, it was hardly noticed by those present.

Rising from her reverence for the rank of her soon-to-be relations, Elizabeth gave a genuine smile to Lady Matlock. In a thrice, the older lady's arms were open. A tiny jingle could be heard as she waved her hands to bid the two Bennet sisters into an embrace as the bracelets on both arms shook.

"My dears, my dears, you have been through too much for lambs." Lady Matlock inspected both of the girls' complexions for signs of fatigue and weariness. Happy with her inspection, she clucked her tongue and tucked an arm of each girl into her own. "For a fortnight it will be my deepest pleasure to erase any pain of your recent past tragedies and show you off as the delightful, intelligent young women I know you to be. Now, tomorrow we will visit the modiste, followed with a short call on Lady Rockford. . ." The Countess of Matlock's voice trailed off as the ladies left the men in the foyer.

"Well, Darce, it looks like we've been replaced." The Colonel gave a guffaw, but his cousin kept his famed mask in place to hide all emotions. "Do not be so dour, Groom. Come, let's join Father in the study." Richard motioned towards the Earl of Matlock, making a hasty exit to the medieval styled, leather upholstered den of retreat for five generations of Fitzwilliam men.

Once the door was shut, the younger men waited for the elder to speak as the Colonel poured drinks. The Earl collapsed into his desk chair and scattered the papers about with a frown on his face. Richard looked to Darcy, who elegantly seated himself in a chair opposite the desk.

"You appear frustrated, Uncle. Is there something I can assist you with?" The Master of Pemberley voice Darcy reserved for formal occasions made an appearance.

"My boy, it's the oldest problem in the kingdom. All the land we cannot need, none of the cash that we do." The Earl continued to seek out a sheet, and finally locating his query, the head of the Fitzwilliam family gave a rare glimpse of his younger self. "Here it is! Richard, come here!"

Already pouring himself another drink, the Colonel flinched, then finished his pour. "Coming, Father." He strode across the study in his full regimentals with the swagger of a war-tested professional.

"I have it here. Visited the blood suckers myself, I did. If you will give up your commission, your grandfather will settle the Grover Downs cottage on you. See, my son, there is no need for you to concern yourself with this black business on the Continent."

"What kind of army man should I consider myself that I did not see this ambush coming, hmm?"

Richard gave his cousin a plaintive look. But Darcy was preoccupied; he sat and watched the swirl of his drink, wondering what his aunt was planning with Elizabeth. He remained completely oblivious as the father and son attempted to speak civilly about their bone of contention, though neither was willing to concede ground.

"I say, in my day, a second son would roll over in mud to have such an offer!"

"And I've tried to tell you father, I am grateful, but this is not my place. Besides, Darcy, you have remained awfully quiet. What say you?"

"Pardon? I fear I was not attending."

"Clearly, Cousin." The Colonel rolled his eyes and took the offer from his father. "Mother's family has joined in the crusade to make me give up my commission." He handed the letter to Darcy and made a prolonged sip of his drink.

The practiced businessman part of Darcy flitted over the broad strokes of the deal, and he absently began to stroke his chin as he often did when ruminating on an idea. "Well, Darce?"

Looking at his uncle and cousin, he was truly neutral. The loyal part of his heart wished nothing more than to support Richard in any scheme the man might dream up. Why, by Jove, he'd even fund it! But the part of his heart that loved his cousin was torn asunder by the very idea of more cannon fire in his general direction. "As no announcement has yet been made about the troops leaving for the Continent, merely blusters of volunteering, perhaps it would be wise to travel this summer to Grover Downs cottage and inspect the property for yourselves. At the very least, if there are any repairs to be made, that can be done should Richard decide the better part of valor is living to fight another day." Darcy handed the letter back to his uncle and stood and bowed. As he moved to exit the room, both men called after him.

With a smile, Darcy turned around. "I'm sorry, gentlemen, but a pair of very fine eyes is owed my presence. I am certain you will remain at a standstill when we next speak."

⚘ ⚘ ⚘ ⚘ ⚘ ⚘ ⚘ ⚘ ⚘

The thread on Jane's shawl twisted mercilessly around her two fingers and she continued her pattern of tightening it and unraveling it to wind it around her fingers again. Lydia was finally asleep, and Kitty was happy to extend her tea to dinner at Darcy House with Georgiana. In her Uncle's sickroom, she sat with her aunt as the three of them discussed what to do about their newest problem.

"We must tell Darcy. He has a right to know." Mr. Gardiner stated, wincing in pain as his leg was still healing from the multiple fractures experienced in the coach accident.

"I still do not see what good that will do. Even should Mr. Wickham be found this very night, my sister is too far gone for there not to be talk. I'm afraid the only option will be to find somewhere to send her away, and . . ," Jane paused as she swallowed once more for the courage of her conviction, "and I shall go with her."

"But where, Jane darling? Where on earth can we send you? I'm afraid we are out of relations. And what of Mr. Bingley? Your absence would be most remarkable."

Jane closed her eyes and pinched her lips together. She breathed in and out of her nose to lessen the aggravation she felt. Once again, that ill-decided courtship was wreaking havoc on her life. Between her and Lydia they were wealthy enough to maintain a household, but there was no way for two unmarried women of marriageable age to do such a thing!

"I know protecting Lydia is your goal, Jane, dear. We just need more options. I still say we need to send for Mr. Darcy." Mr. Gardiner coughed and whooped in pain. His broken ribs on the same side of his leg injury were irritated with his talking and Mrs. Gardiner rushed forward to grab her husband's hand lest he thrash in response to the pain. After a moment, Mr. Gardiner regained his composure and with teary eyes, he whispered thanks to his wife.

"No."

Both of the Gardiners turned to the shocking firmness in Jane's voice.

"There will be no bothering Fitzwilliam or Elizabeth so close to their wedding. They both deserve one brief period of happiness before the ugliness of this business is bandied about." Jane rose from her chair. "I know what must be done. On the morrow, I will take the carriage to Matlock house and request an audience with the Colonel. If there is any help to be found in that quarter, he is the right man to approach."

Jane nodded to both of her relations and quit the room to check on Lydia. As she left and quietly shut the door, Mrs. Gardiner turned her attentions back to her husband. With a light pressure, she kissed his forehead and locked eyes with him.

"That's two now that are all grown up. When did it happen, Edward? How did we miss it?"

Taking a measured breath, Mr. Gardiner managed the only response he could. "God is gracious."

Chapter Twelve

Elizabeth returned from her unfashionable morning walk in Hyde Park to see her older sister exiting the Matlock study with Colonel Fitzwilliam.

"Jane!" Elizabeth rushed forward to hug her sister. "Is anything the matter? Aunt? I knew I should have called the doctor last time!"

Bewildered, Jane looked at the Colonel, then back to her sister. "No, no, everything is fine. What is this about Aunt?"

Frowning, Elizabeth was still flushed from her exercise, and her hunger was increasing a notch. "She said it was normal pain, her body adjusting. . . but I thought . . ." Elizabeth looked to the Colonel who was admiring a perfectly shined suit of armor and realized this discussion was not appropriate. Lady Matlock descended the stairs to find both Bennet sisters and her son.

"Lovely, Miss Bennet, you have come. See, I knew she would be willing to shop; all women are." Lady Matlock took her son's arm to be escorted into the dining room to break her fast.

"Lizzie . . .," Jane whispered. "What is Lady Matlock talking about?"

"Ssshh, I was going to give your regrets, but now it is too late. Smile, you're going to the modiste."

"But it's so expensive!" Jane frowned as she did not wish to spend more money on dresses when she might very well need her savings, and Lydia's, to keep the family safe, once, that is, either Mr. Wickham was found or a living arrangement could be found from the Colonel.

"Why ever did you come this morning?" Elizabeth asked, but they were interrupted by the Colonel returning to fetch them.

"Ladies, I believe your presence is required." He smiled and gave Miss Bennet a wink behind Elizabeth's back. Jane nodded to the gentleman, thankful for his interference, but not sure how long she was going to be able to keep hiding secrets from her favorite sister. Her original plan was to avoid Lizzie's presence as much as possible, and on the very first day she had failed miserably.

After another pin-pricking, dress-shopping expedition, the ladies of Matlock House and guests found a pretty little pastry shop on the Promenade for refreshment. They had just made their order when Mr. Darcy arrived, much to the happiness of Elizabeth.

"And were we successful in new silks and satins to wear?" Darcy looked to Miss Mary for an answer, and the young woman smiled.

"Indeed, and Lizzie and Jane even talked me into short sleeves!" The table shared a laugh, and Lady Matlock began a conversation with Jane and Mary to give the couple a small amount of privacy in public.

"Did you meet with Mr. Adams? Was he able to draft all of the paperwork?" Elizabeth asked Mr.

Darcy in earnest. He nodded.

"It was a smooth transaction."

Jane's ear pricked up at the talk of money transfers. "What paperwork? I thought your marriage settlement was signed weeks ago."

"Of course, of course, Miss Bennet. This was a new scheme devised by the lovely future Mrs. Darcy. I was only happy to be a party."

Elizabeth sighed and shook her head. "He's being much too modest. I simply asked Mr. Darcy to arrange to send my dowry back to the Gardiners to help tide them over. Uncle will be out of work for nearly six months, and this is a safety net."

"Though I, and my best men, will stay on top of the business to ensure inventory is handled properly." Mr. Darcy clarified.

Lady Matlock cleared her throat, looking around at the members of London society beginning to pay attention to their very inappropriate subject of money and trade. "Have you heard that Hamlet opens next week? The delay has been most dreadful, but when your Ophelia falls ill, you can not very well allow the show to go on. Darcy, you should take Elizabeth and the Miss Bennets! Opening night will be the perfect time for that golden dress, my dear. You'll make all of the other debutantes green with envy."

"I had planned to take Miss Elizabeth as a surprise, Aunt Maggie."

Elizabeth looked down at her lap, saddened that poor William's plans were spoiled. Her insides twisted at the care that he would have to surprise her thus, and she only looked up when she realized Jane was speaking.

"Mr. Bingley mentioned the theater, but I had

yet to give him an answer."

"Oh, not the odious Bingleys. Such upstarts," Lady Matlock frowned, "I'm terribly sorry, but that sister of his with her strong perfumes and unconscionable fashion choices. I will not attend if they are to join the party."

"Bingley is my oldest friend. They can sit in the Darcy box."

"That is certainly fine, but you and Miss Elizabeth and the Bennet sisters will sit in the Matlock box. It is time to begin Elizabeth's acceptance into society after the ruckus Catherine caused."

"Kitty? What has my sister done?" Jane asked, sweetly with concern.

"No, dear, not the younger, my sister-in-law. Lady Catherine was most vexing at a few events at the Carrigans', not that I ever accept her invitations. Her father was in trade and she made a marriage of convenience for a title. And from what I've heard, Miss Bingley was not singing any of your praises, either. I would be very careful around that one."

The sour taste of bile rose up Darcy's esophagus. He had warned Charles about his sister, but apparently it had fallen on deaf ears. "I shall not extend the invitation to Charles."

Saddened further, Elizabeth reached under the table and squeezed Darcy's hand, causing him to look at her with such loneliness in his eyes, a loneliness he only showed her. As Jane sat next to Elizabeth, she caught the brief exchange between the couple and doubled her resolve to keep Lydia's situation from the rest of the family.

"Mr. Darcy, with all of the engagements you and Elizabeth will need to attend, might not Georgiana appreciate an extended visit from Kitty? I hate to impose . . ."

"It's no imposition What a wonderful idea, Miss Bennet! Why had I not thought to put the two young ladies together? After all, I will be sponsoring them both next Season." Darcy could already see the wheels turning in his aunt's mind.

"As my aunt says, it is no imposition, and I will ask Georgiana's tutors to begin an evaluation of Miss Catherine. Perhaps this summer she can reside with Georgiana here in London and improve her mind."

"Oh, Mr. Darcy, I'm not so sure about that. Kitty has never been too keen to learn. . ."

"That was before, Lizzie, but she's changed. She has greatly improved her mind with writing, and I'm certain she would relish the opportunity to learn more." Mary spoke up.

"Then it's settled. I shall send a note this afternoon to have her packed and sent to Darcy House." Lady Matlock beamed at her growing little family at the table.

"There's no need, milady. I will share the invitation when I return." Jane smiled and received a glowing smile in return.

After the refreshments were enjoyed, the parties separated with Mr. Darcy offering Jane a ride home in his carriage, which she readily accepted. It was the one time Elizabeth found herself to be slightly jealous of her sister.

❧ ❧ ❧ ❧ ❧ ❧ ❧ ❧ ❧

While most of the household rested for a night out at the ball held by the Cornish family, Elizabeth had escaped to the library to find a prayer book. She was not very far when she was joined in the library by the Earl.

"My lord," she curtsied as she saw him enter.

"Can we dispense with all this curtsying? I am to be your uncle, my dear. How about Uncle Reginald when it's just family, eh? We don't use the Fitzwilliam name for obvious reasons . . .," he said with a smirk. Reginald Fitzwilliam walked to his future niece and took her by both hands and squeezed them. "I must give you thanks for all of the time and energy you have bestowed upon my wife. Did she ever tell you that we had three daughters?"

Elizabeth looked perplexed. She had only heard of the Viscount, who was away until the engagement ball to oversee planting at Matlock, and the Colonel. "I don't understand my lo- Uncle Reginald."

"All perished in 1798, much like your papa more recently. It was a sudden fever, all of the children had it. We prayed and prayed, but only our eldest boys survived." Lord Matlock looked to a painting on the far wall that clearly showed three young girls playing on a swing. "My oldest, Anne Marie, would have been twenty-two this year."

"I'm so very sorry you lost your daughters."

Inhaling through his nose, the Earl seemed to get his emotions under better regulation and took a look at the book in Elizabeth's hands. "And here I am interrupting your prayers. Forgive me. . .," He nodded and turned to walk away, but Elizabeth stopped him.

"Please don't leave. I confess I was not praying."

"Oh?" the Earl was intrigued. "Is that not what most persons do with a prayer book?"

Elizabeth giggled, reminded of how her father

would have questioned her silliness. "Yes, sir, but I am here for a much more selfish reason." The Earl motioned for her to continue. "I have never been to an actual wedding, and I wished to read the ceremony so that I might be familiar with the proceedings. I would hate to embarrass William or Lady Matlock by stumbling through my own."

The Earl laughed, a deep belly laugh, and Elizabeth found the sentiment contagious. "My dear, my dear, I have sat through enough stuffy, high society weddings to last a lifetime! Why, in the months of July and August, there seem to be two or three a week! I shall be happy to walk you through the ceremony."

And so the Earl explained to Elizabeth all of the finer, salient points of the ceremony and played the vicar's role in asking her to recite her vows. Once they were finished, Elizabeth thanked him for all of his assistance and was ready to retire to her room when the Earl asked her one last question.

"Miss Elizabeth, I know you might not have thought about this, but with your uncle bedridden, had you considered who would walk you down the aisle?"

An intense wave of melancholy washed over Elizabeth's heart, and the temporary jubilation she felt from laughing and learning with the Earl disappeared. She had thought to simply walk herself to William when the time came, without her father, what else was to be done, and she told the Earl such. He held up his hand. "I respect your wishes, and certainly understand if that is what you still choose, but after all that I have heard and witnessed of your spirit and candor, I would be truly honored to walk you down the aisle to marry my nephew."

Tears sprung to Elizabeth's eyes, and without a second thought she bounded up and tackled poor Lord Matlock with a hug. "Dear, dear, careful with these old bones."

Wiping her eyes, she beamed at the man. "I would love to have your escort, sir." And she curtsied low.

"Now, now, we dispensed with that."

"I know, but you deserved it." Elizabeth gave him a minxish smile before leaving the study, prayer book in tow so she could study her lines some more. As the door closed, Reginald Fitzwilliam took one more look at his girls on the wall and thanked God in heaven for bringing his family young ladies who needed them.

ぷ ぷ ぷ ぷ ぷ ぷ ぷ ぷ ぷ

By the night of the opening for Hamlet, poor Jane was weary and wrecked. Her mother had not tarried long behind Lydia. All of the Gardiner household was in an uproar. Despite her best intentions, she was at a loss to control both her mother and Lydia and their demands on the household staff while Mrs. Gardiner was increasing and Mr. Gardiner still recuperated. That the engagement ball was only two nights away, and the wedding the following morning, tonight's event was the one of the last she would have to endure, then she would find a safe place to keep Lydia.

As the Darcy carriage arrived, Jane tried to leave right away, but Elizabeth rushed into the household against Jane's wishes. "I want Aunt to see my dress! I promised her. . ." but Elizabeth's jaw dropped as soon as she reached the foyer to see a very plump Lydia in the drawing room with her mother.

"Oh, Lizzie, what jewels! Did Mr. Darcy give them to you? Oh, I just knew he would be so kind. Ever so kind!" Mrs. Bennet rushed from her chair and approached Elizabeth to touch the large canary diamond hanging around her neck. Behind her, Mr. Darcy entered the home and stepped back as it appeared Mrs. Bennet was rushing right at them, and then he too spied the horror.

"Wickham" he hissed, causing Elizabeth to turn her head, almost yanking her necklace out of her mother's hands.

"Come now, we must not be late. The show begins soon. Mother, I will be sure to tell you all when I return."

"It's not fair! Kitty gets to go! Mama, make them take me with."

"Sssshhh, Lyddie, darling. Mama needs you to stay and play some cards. Yes, I would love a good game of gin." Mrs. Bennet turned to tend to her youngest daughter while the older daughters and Mr. Darcy made their escape.

"How could you? This is what you have been hiding! I knew you had a secret." Elizabeth's anger pierced Jane's heart as she began to cry. "Don't give me your tears, I know how to work a good cry, too. This is vile, Jane!"

"I know! I know! But you and Mr. Darcy were so happy. . . and I couldn't . . ."

"Ladies, perchance we could discuss this in the carriage?" Darcy's voice was flat, and a stab of fear gripped Elizabeth's heart. What if? What if he cancelled their wedding now that Lydia was carrying Wickham's bastard child? Seeming to interpret Elizabeth's thoughts, Mr. Darcy squeezed her hand as he saw her into the carriage. "I will never abandon you," was all he said, but it was enough.

Once settled in the carriage and thankful that Mary had ridden with the Matlocks, Elizabeth began her inquisition again. "How long have you known? Since Uncle was injured?"

"No, no, but well, now I know there were signs even back when you and Mr. Darcy were still in the neighborhood. It wasn't until the babe moved that Lydia took the post to London, the same day you left for the Matlocks."

Darcy groaned at the intelligence of how far along the development was as his plan to marry Lydia off flew out the window. "Who else is aware of your sister's condition?"

Jane bit her lip. "The Gardiners and Mama. And also your cousin, Colonel Fitzwilliam."

"Richard knows of this?"

Jane nodded. "He was looking for Mr. Wickham, and after you were married, he was going to help me find a country home where Lydia and I can raise the baby."

"And you didn't tell me and William because you feared he would call off the wedding," Elizabeth finished.

"Not exactly," Jane looked to an affronted Mr. Darcy. "I never thought Mr. Darcy would give you up, but I was afraid the wedding might be postponed on account of Lydia, and you both were so happy. I am the oldest. It was my responsibility to handle it."

Looking at the two sisters, Darcy had to admit

he was impressed. Most ladies of the ton would be crying hysterically, but here were two ladies using cool and calm logic to handle their problems. He took a deep breath as he noticed they were nearing the theater. "Ladies, it's time we put on a brave face, or the vultures out there will sniff something is amiss. Jane, I must say you did an admirable job in trying to protect your family."

Jane smiled and sat up a little straighter on the bench she shared with Elizabeth. "Thank you, Mr. Darcy. Please, call me Jane."

Despite the gravity of the situation, Mr. Darcy gave his future sister-in-law a rare show of his dimpled smile. It was short lived though as he donned his mask of indifference the second the carriage door opened. As he handed Elizabeth out of the carriage after assisting Jane, he made sure to scrunch his nose, causing his beloved to laugh. It was just the kind of arrival that the mavens of London society expected to see of a love match, and only the truly vicious members with an axe to grind against Lady Matlock continued their scrutiny for cracks in the veneer.

By the time the couple of the evening made it to the Matlock box, Elizabeth's hand ached from so many introductions. If she had to say "How do you do?" or answer that her father had owned a small estate in Hertfordshire but had passed last fall one more time, she was going to start yanking headpieces and stomping on slippers. Taking a calming breath, she steadied her nerves as Kitty and Georgiana began pointing and whispering next to her.

"Girls, what is it? You do realize all in the theater can see us?" The two young girls suddenly froze, becoming extremely self-conscious as the truth of Elizabeth's words sunk in.

"Mr. Bingley sits over there with two women and not by his sister. She is sitting with that charming fellow, laughing, and touching his arm all over." Kitty handed Elizabeth her theater glasses so she could see. Stunned, Elizabeth indeed saw Mr. Bingley openly entertaining two women she had yet to meet, but recalled seeing at the Matlocks' Twelfth Night ball. Frantic, she turned her head to look at Jane sitting one seat over, only to get a close up of her older sister already looking at the box across from them with her own spectacles.

"Jane, . . ." Elizabeth started, but Mr. Darcy returned with the refreshments, and the lights darkened in the house.

"What is the matter?" Darcy whispered. Elizabeth exchanged the refreshments for the opera glasses and told him to look at Bingley in the box across the way. A small curse could be heard under his breath.

"Jane," he whispered, "this is my fault, and I feel beastly. I never told Charles we were attending the theater tonight."

"Mr. Darcy, Charles invited me to this performance the day Lydia arrived. I never gave an answer. That he has found other friends to enjoy the performance, I am happy about. Please, make nothing of this."

As Elizabeth could hear the words coming out of Jane's mouth, she also could hear the intense sorrow behind each syllable. If she had the strength to lob something hard across the playhouse and hit Mr. Bingley in the head, he'd be enjoying an intense headache at the moment. But she wasn't eight years old anymore when she could throw rocks at the boys being mean to Jane. Between Lydia and now Bingley, the night was completely ruined, and she had so wished to enjoy this play. The only relief she had was watching Georgiana and Kitty, giddy with excitement, oblivious to the very real threats to their family's good standing.

Chapter Thirteen

The engagement ball of Fitzwilliam Darcy to Elizabeth Bennet was the social event of the Season thus far. Every room in the Matlock townhouse seemed to burst at the seams as everyone who knew anyone had weaseled their way in. Of course, Lady Matlock had instructed the footmen to stop checking the guest list after supper so that all might see the future Mrs. Darcy in all of her splendor. As far as ladies were concerned, a ballroom was a battlefield, and Margaret Elizabeth Fitzwilliam took no prisoners.

Elizabeth enjoyed her second dance with Mr. Darcy, having danced the supper set with his cousin the Viscount. Both Elizabeth and Darcy had complained about this ploy by his aunt, but she was adamant that Elizabeth receive proper attention by all of the titled men in the room. Eventually, both had given up their arguments.

As the couples grew close for a part of the dance, Lady Carrigan stood gossiping with Caroline Bingley, who when not gaining a request to dance after the second set had claimed an ankle injury and was lounging on a sofa against the wall.

"I say, what is that vulgar thing they are doing with their noses?" Lady Amelia Carrigan sniffed the air and pursed her lips.

"It's probably that Bennet chit's fault. Her entire family is vulgar, and she's used her arts and allurements to pervert poor Mr. Darcy." Caroline Bingley scowled, wishing she could stand up and survey the dancers, but she couldn't give up the ruse of her ankle injury. "When we were in Hertfordshire, did you know that all five of the sisters are out?"

"All five? How absurd!"

"Yes, and the youngest was engaged this winter to a Mr. Wickham, but he left a great deal of debt and deserted the militia. It was quite the scandal." By now, a number of other ladies nearby were craning their necks to listen in with a look of indifference. Caroline Bingley waited for the coup de grace, knowing if she didn't do this correctly, all would be for naught.

"And where is this sister? I see only four of the Bennets." Mrs. Courtney chimed in, asking the question most of the women in earshot all wanted to ask.

"Oh, she's in town, staying with the aunt and uncle in trade. Big as a whale." Caroline smiled as the ladies around her all gasped. Applause broke out as the song ended, and the couples left the dance floor. Of course, all it took was the hustle and bustle of such a change in music for the gossip group to fan out in the ballroom.

Elizabeth smiled at William as he helped her to the punch bowl. The heat of the room and recent activity made her cheeks glow, and Darcy leaned forward to whisper how beautiful and tempting she looked. Elizabeth was just turning away in embarrassment, feeling slight trepidation for the morning's ceremony, when she came face to face with the Earl. He bowed low and kissed her hand.

"Might I have this next dance, my dear?"

Elizabeth handed her cup to Darcy, who grinned shamelessly at his bride. "Yes, you may."

As the Earl escorted Elizabeth to the dance floor, she noticed the entire ballroom seemed to be whispering at such a courtesy and pointedly looking at her. As the first notes of a Scottish reel began to play, Elizabeth twirled and linked arms with her new uncle in the complicated movements. She spun and worked her way down the line, catching brief glimpses of the angry faces and frowns. The music continued to play, and the dance continued, but Elizabeth's head continuously turned in opposite directions of her movements as she tried to understand what was going on.

Once she spun down the far line and returned to Lord Matlock, she noticed his face was also grim and strained.

"Has Lady Catherine stormed the ball a second time?" she asked, almost out of breath, still looking around her. The Earl clasped hands with her for the fastest spin yet. Just before it was over, he grunted that he was unaware of the problem at hand.

Despite wishing nothing more than to stop, as her supper was beginning to slosh and bash against the insides of her stomach, Elizabeth soldiered on and completed her second circuit down the line, spinning and twirling with each man in the set. Once the nightmarish dance was over, the Earl escorted Elizabeth with his head held high, and the entire ballroom was nearly silent aside from whispers.

They arrived at Lady Matlock looking agitated, standing with Mr. Darcy and Lady Cornish and Lady Carrigan.

"It would appear that a most vicious rumor has been spread about your youngest sister, Lydia, dear, that she is not in attendance tonight due to being heavy with child."

Elizabeth laughed heartily, truly imaging the plump Lydia trying to accomplish the dance she just finished, so it had a genuine ring to it. "Forgive me, oh, but I need refreshment. Lord Matlock is spritely on his feet." Elizabeth smiled and played her part as the Earl bowed and offered to retrieve her drink as any gallant dance partner would. Elizabeth happily linked arms with Mr. Darcy and smiled up at him, then she turned her attention to Lady Carrigan. "I'm sorry, we were discussing Lydia? You do know she's just a girl of fifteen. It would hardly be appropriate for her to dance on an evening such as this."

"Miss Bingley says she danced with all of the officers at numerous balls in Meryton. That she is engaged to a Mr. Wickham."

"Well, of course in our home county my parents did indulge her a bit to let her practice. But you will see my sister Catherine does not dance this evening, along with Miss Darcy. And they are both older than Lydia."

"Yes, but why then is she not present? If you wish for her to have all of this practice as you call it, surely you'd wish her to observe a true London ball." Lady Cornish looked down her nose at Elizabeth, positively salivating for a mistake. But Elizabeth held her gaze and never once looked to Lady Matlock for assistance, something both titled ladies were counting upon.

"My father passed away only this past autumn. My mother, recently widowed, had a brother gravely injured in a carriage accident not two months ago. My sister Lydia, being the youngest and Mama's favorite, is a great comfort. My mother suffers from bouts of nerves ,and at times, it's only Lydia who can calm her."

Satisfied with their intelligence, the ladies were about to saunter off when Lady Matlock stopped them. "I am certain you will be happy to spread how wonderful Lydia Bennet is as a comfort to her dear mother just as fastidiously as you were to spread the lies of her being with child. After all, we can hardly trust those new to our circle with the stench of new money. They'll say practically anything to gain status." Lady Matlock made a pointed look at Miss Bingley, who was at that very moment being roughly assisted off the sofa by two footmen and escorted out of the ballroom.

Elizabeth dropped her jaw in shock, continuing her part in pretending how absurd the entire fiasco had become. Caroline, catching Elizabeth's eye, and seeing her smirk for just a moment before resuming her facade, lost her composure. "I saw her! She's round with child, I tell you. My sister just had a babe, I know what it looks like!" Mr. Bingley watched in horror as his sister was escorted out, bowed to the few companions he was speaking to and followed her cries.

Lady Matlock pressed her lips together and looked at her two social enemies. "See what I mean? Cannot even observe proper decorum in a ballroom . . . Elizabeth darling, have you met the Duke and

Duchess of Derby? Come, they've been asking to see you and Darcy all evening." And with that, Lady Matlock whisked her nephew and his intended off to the opposite end of the ballroom, exhibiting her Napoleonic skills at social warfare.

Nearly three in the morning, the last couple left the town home and Elizabeth had long since planned to retire. After all, she was to be married in just a few hours. Instead, she had remained awake because the very real problem of Lydia still needed to be decided. All of London would now be looking to see Lydia at the wedding and her size would surely set tongues wagging once more. As Elizabeth sat up with William and his aunt and uncle, they were all stumped at how they were going to hide her in plain sight.

Tears and exhaustion began to overtake Elizabeth and Mr. Darcy insisted his bride retire. "But, my sister! We are ruined. I have ruined you!"

"Ssssh, if we must run away to Gretna Green then so be it, but I am marrying you, Elizabeth Bennet, in . . ." Darcy looked at the clock on the mantle, "eight hours."

Giving him a weak smile, Elizabeth retired to her room with Lady Matlock accompanying her. As they climbed the stairs together, the older woman tried to calm Elizabeth.

"My son is a brilliant tactician. If anyone can devise a ruse, it is he."

In spite of herself, Elizabeth laughed. "Well, at least my sister's tragedy distracts from any wedding nerves!"

Lady Matlock frowned and paused in the hallway with Elizabeth. "Dear, I assumed your aunt would discuss these things with you, but do you have any worries or fears about what happens after the wedding ceremony?"

Elizabeth shook her head and answered that her Aunt Gardiner had addressed the topic already. Wishing each other a good night, Lady Matlock squeezed Elizabeth's hand in affection before excusing herself to the family wing. As Elizabeth collapsed into the fluffy bed, she was too tired to even finish her thought about it being her last night as a Bennet.

❧ ❧ ❧ ❧ ❧ ❧ ❧ ❧ ❧

At the sound of Becky moving about, Elizabeth's eyes sprang open. Today she was to be married! She looked down and realized she had not only slept in her ball gown from last night, but also the beautiful jewelry that Mr. Darcy had given her.

"No worries, miss. A hot bath is at the ready." Becky helped Elizabeth take off the jewels and place them in a new lockable travel jewelry chest, an early wedding gift from the Matlocks. Wide awake in anticipation, Elizabeth spied unfamiliar trunks in the room.

"Becky, whose luggage is in my room?"

The maid looked at Elizabeth suspiciously, knowing her mistress was one of the brightest women in all of England, or so she told the other servants. "Why, they be yours, ma'am."

"But there's too many!"

Becky shook her head. "No, Miss Elizabeth, each time you visited the modiste, the Countess and Mr. Darcy used your measurements to have a whole trousseau and winter wardrobe made. Said Scotland can still be a dash cold this time of year."

Elizabeth groaned and allowed herself to be steered to the bathing room adjacent to her guest suite that she shared with Mary. Additional maids were already present, and Elizabeth experienced a bath like no other. No sooner had one washed her hair that another was working on her nails, while still another scrubbed a foot. She felt pulled and pushed in all different directions. For a moment, she worried that with the maids working silently they might accidentally drown her!

Wrapped in a number of bathing towels, Elizabeth donned a new chemise and sat in the chair in front of her dressing table. Briefly she caught glimpses of her wild curls as two maids rubbed her head to dry her hair. Next, with Becky working the brush through the tangles she sat squinting and yelping at the pain.

"I'm sorry, miss, but we are a little behind schedule." Becky apologized, knowing Elizabeth was very tender headed. Elizabeth sighed and understood, forcing her thoughts to William as she endured the torture.

Two hours later a knock at the door caused the maids to all disappear, aside from Becky, who merely answered and stayed back. The Earl of Matlock, in full aristocratic regalia, entered, causing Elizabeth to tear up as looking in her mirror, she watched him walk into the room.. As he reached her, she turned, and he handed her a handkerchief.

"Maggie said you would need this!" He laughed, causing Elizabeth to laugh as well.

The ride to church was a short one, and the

streets of Mayfair were eerily quiet. It appeared all had crowded into St. Paul's Cathedral to see the wedding of the Season. For years, the matrons of London had tried and failed to snare the most wealthy and eligible Mr. Darcy, and in the end, it was a slip of a country miss who trapped his heart. All heads turned as Elizabeth walked down the aisle with the Earl of Matlock proudly escorting his future niece.

Mr. Darcy attempted to be the last to see his bride sweep down the aisle, but his best man clapped him on the shoulder. "Turn around, man. Your future happiness is splendid." As Darcy turned, his breath caught, and the rest of the church appeared to blur around him as he only saw Elizabeth, his Elizabeth, walking towards him in a gown of lavender silk, with small purple buds and pearls in her hair. He watched each breath make her décolletage rise and fall before following the graceful lines of her neck to her perfect rose-colored lips. Unconsciously wetting his own lips as they suddenly felt very dry, his eyes locked with hers, and he felt his heart lighten.

The bishop performed the ceremony admirably, and Elizabeth managed to repeat her vows in a clear, strong voice, never taking her eyes off William. For his part, he also performed perfectly, oblivious to any and all around them. As the bishop's final command was said, it was Fitzwilliam's greatest pleasure to tilt Elizabeth's chin up with his hand and lean in to kiss her most passionately, to the deafening cheers of the church around them.

As Darcy grabbed Elizabeth's hand to walk with her down the aisle, she struggled to keep up with him. She tried to smile and nod at their guests, but they were in the narthex before she could catch her breath.

"William! The rush?"

"We must hurry or the plan will fail. Here, sign the registry." A few guests began to exit the church and crowd them. Elizabeth signed her new name, wishing she had prepared more for this step, and hastily followed her husband outside.

A carriage with all of her new trunks strapped to it awaited at the end of the steps. Darcy wasted no time rushing Elizabeth down the steps, opened the carriage door so that a female occupant inside could be seen slightly by the guests billowing outside. He grabbed Elizabeth by the waist to pull her in for one last passionate kiss, to the catcalls of many, before assisting her inside the carriage. Leaning out, he waved and shut the door, banging for the carriage to begin its journey.

Inside, Elizabeth was surprised to see Lydia, bawling her eyes out, sitting in the carriage with them. She looked to Mr. Darcy for an explanation, but he merely smiled and nodded. "I suppose we are skipping the wedding breakfast?" she asked lifting her eyebrows for the first time as Mrs. Darcy.

Without an answer, Mr. Darcy just continued to smile like the cat that swallowed the canary.

The chaos and confusion reigned supreme in the milling guests. Those who witnessed the passionate abduction of Mrs. Darcy by Mr. Darcy didn't fail to recount the story again and again for those who had missed the escape. The Colonel merely had to mention there was someone else in the carriage for the explanation that Lydia Bennet was not at the ceremony because she was working with William on his little scheme to escape with his bride for the honeymoon in Scotland, which she was invited to join long ago, to take hold. The Matlocks hosted the finest wedding breakfast without the bride and groom present ever seen, and the ton of London were quite satisfied with the spectacle.

It was only Jane Bennet who remained behind after the guests had dispersed to ask for an audience with the Colonel in the library. As the Colonel agreed to her request, he braced himself for what he knew was coming.

"Explain to me how I was shuffled aside for the care of Lydia? She is my sister, and I demand to know where she is going and what is to be her fate!" Jane Bennet's wrath was a sight to behold. Even the Colonel had to take a step back in marvel.

"Peace, Miss Bennet. After the rumors at the ball started by Caroline Bingley, we had to take desperate action. Lydia is safe and on her way to Scotland, under the protection of Elizabeth and Darcy."

Jane scrunched up her fists and stomped her foot. "No! That is expressly what I did not want! This is my burden to bear. It is I who should have curtailed her behavior and stayed with Mama when we came to London."

In Jane's rage, she had not heard Lady Matlock enter the library, nor the grand lady's approach.

"Jane, dear, may I call you Jane?" Her voice was calm and steady, in order to soothe the irate young woman before her. Jane's features softened, and she took a few steadying breaths, mortified at the loss of her temper. "Lydia will have the best care, the best midwife in Scotland. All has been arranged. But to keep her safe, we do need your help."

Jane brightened and stood up straighter. "Anything. I will take the next post carriage to Scotland if need be."

Lady Matlock smiled at the gumption of the young woman. Were all of the Bennets born with such bravery? "At the moment, your rushing off to Scotland would rather set off alarms that there was something amiss, and we do not want that, do we?" Jane nodded. "No, I will need you and Mary to join me this summer in dazzling our critics. A united front! We will smile and dance at every soiree and keep building the status and significance of the Bennet name."

The smile on Jane's face melted. "You mean, stay in London? With you, here?"

Lady Matlock smiled and, with a sparkle in her eye, rubbed the upper arms of her newest prote'gee'. "We can visit the modiste this afternoon." She clucked her tongue and swished out of the library just as silently as she had arrived, leaving the door wide open.

Jane stood there, her mouth gaped open, staring at the empty doorway. The Colonel felt it safe enough to move closer to the young woman.

"She's a bit scary, isn't she?" He laughed at his own joke as Jane just nodded. "Well, buck up private. You're in the Matlock army now." He gave a pert pat to Jane's back and walked away from her with his arms behind his back, just as he would after inspecting a line.

Left in the library alone, Jane Bennet began to shake as the full consequences of her actions and agreements swirled in her mind. She gingerly sat on the nearest chair, wondering how on earth she was going to manage a social calendar the likes of Lady Matlock had planned for her while concealing such a deep shame. Worse, who was going to convince Mrs. Bennet to go back to Hertfordshire?

The sounds of the Matlock servants restoring the household snapped Jane out of her introspection. Shoulders back, head held high, she glided out of the library, thinking of the fierceness she had seen Elizabeth display time and time again. If her sister could sacrifice her honeymoon to conceal Lydia's predicament, then Jane would bravely sacrifice one summer in society.

ABOUT THE AUTHOR

Elizabeth Ann West is a jane-of-all-trades, mistress to none. Author of the best-selling women's fiction, *Cancelled*, and historical romance series *Seasons of Serendipity*, she began her writing career in 2007 writing advertising copy for websites. Since then, she has learned to make apps, code websites, and make a mean cup of coffee. Originally from Virginia Beach, VA, her family now moves wherever the Navy sends them.

You can contact her at

writer@elizabethannwest.com

Or join her **Pemberley Possibilities** mailing list:

http://bit.ly/emailpemberley

You can read more works by Elizabeth and keep up with her latest news at:

elizabethannwest.com

77345237R00099

Made in the USA
Columbia, SC
23 September 2017